I0592686

An Australian Girl in London

LOUISE MACK (MRS J. P. CREED)

with an introduction by SARAH POPE

Grattan Street Press

Grattan Street Press is the imprint of the
teaching press based in the School of Culture and
Communication at the University of Melbourne,
Parkville, Australia.

THE UNIVERSITY OF
MELBOURNE

Cover Image
Arthur Streeton (1867-1943)
Cremorne 1895
Oil on wood
Gift of Howard Hinton 1934
The Howard Hinton Collection
New England Regional Art Museum

An Australian Girl in London originally published in 1902 by
T. Fisher Unwin in London

Grattan Street Press
School of Culture and Communication
John Medley Building,
Parkville, VIC 3010
www.grattanstreetpress.com

Printed in Australia

NATIONAL
LIBRARY
OF AUSTRALIA

A catalogue record for this
book is available from the
National Library of Australia

SERIES INTRODUCTION

The Colonial Australian Popular Fiction series brings the excitement and diversity of colonial Australian fiction to the attention of contemporary readers – and there is certainly some remarkable fiction to read here.

Encompassing both novels and short-story collections, the series will include a range of popular genres that flourished during the colonial period: the bush sketch, the Lemurian novel, crime and detective fiction, the colonial romance, the Gothic tale, the convict novel, the goldfields adventure, and the bushranger novel. Some of the authors were bestsellers in their day, and their work can still take us by surprise. We aim to make colonial Australian fiction accessible to contemporary readers – and we hope the design and layout of these works will be helpful here.

But we also want to honour the original forms of these works. So we have reprinted from first editions or from the original serialisation of a work in newspapers or journals. Each publication includes a short introduction written by academic specialists, which provides a brief biography of the author (or authors) and offers critical insight into the work and its contexts. We would be particularly pleased if some of our publications eventually became set texts in university or senior secondary courses. We believe these vibrant works from our turbulent past have much to offer all readers of Australian literature. Some of them – especially those exploring the colonial frontier – can be confronting in the intensity of their racism and the level of their violence against Aboriginal people. But it is important for contemporary Australians to experience the legacies of colonialism in all their dark complexity. By doing so, we can begin to understand our historical condition and work towards a more reconciled future.

The *Colonial Australian Popular Fiction* series is an ongoing collaboration between the Grattan Street Press and the Australian Centre, both based within the School of Culture and Communication at the University of Melbourne.

Ken Gelder and Rachael Weaver

CONTENTS

Introduction	IX
A Note on the Text	XIX
An Australian Girl in London	1
Grattan Street Press Personnel	182
Acknowledgements	183
About the Australian Centre	186
About Grattan Street Press	187

INTRODUCTION

Sarah Pope

Louise Mack's *An Australian Girl in London* (1902) is an epistolary novel that follows the literal and literary journey of its fictional heroine, Sylvia Leighton, who travels via steamship from Australia to Britain. One could be forgiven for thinking that this novel tells the story of Mack herself, who made the same journey in 1901 to become an Australian girl in London just after the turn of the century. Marie Louise Hamilton Mack was born in Hobart, Tasmania on 10 October 1870. She was the first daughter – and 'the central figure of a family of thirteen' – of Rev. Hans Hamilton Mack, a Wesleyan minister from Ireland, and Jemima Mack, née James, an educated woman from Northern Ireland.[1] Mack was greatly influenced by her parents and according to one account, 'owe[d] much of her development to her mother's literary tastes, and the varied training that an intellectual father can bestow on his children'.[2] Her parents encouraged her to read and write poetry, which she did from a very young age, as did her younger sister Amy, who became a prolific writer of children's stories and poetry.

Mack's early childhood was spent travelling between the Australian colonies, thanks to the precarious nature of her father's religious obligations. In 1883, when she was twelve, Mack moved to Sydney with her family, where they first lived in Balmain and then moved frequently within the inner west, between Newtown and Redfern. In 1885 she began attending the Sydney Girls High School with her younger sisters Alice, Florence, Amy and Gertrude. Here she was a contemporary of the Australian literary

---

[1] 'Miss A. Louise Mack', *Methodist*, 23 November 1895, p.1.

[2] Ibid.

icon, Ethel Turner, author of *Seven Little Australians* (1894). Mack and Turner were at once best friends and keen rivals, their competitive relationship lasting throughout their schooling and subsequent literary careers. Perhaps because of this, Mack became intensely prolific and was early on considered a 'rising … star' within the Australian literary community.[3] As the editor of the Sydney Girls High School literary magazine, the *Gazette*, she chose to decline a number of Turner's submissions. Turner responded by starting her own literary magazine, the *Iris*, with her sister Lilian, another novelist and writer of children's fiction. Mack recounted these school experiences and reflected on her friendship and rivalry with Turner in her early novels *Teens: A Story of Australian School Girls* (1897) and *Girls Together* (1898), both published by Angus & Robertson. Yet despite her early literary relationships and accomplishments, Mack's fortunes as a serious literary figure in Australia soon dwindled. She was referred to, often pejoratively, as a writer of romance fiction: her novels were written *about* Australian girls *for* Australian girls.

Much to her disappointment Mack did not matriculate and was forced to move to the country and work as a governess after leaving school. Despite loathing her job, it was during this time that she 'developed an almost mystical love for the Australian countryside'.[4] She was a regular contributor to the *Bulletin* and was eventually appointed as a member of staff, writing the 'Woman's Letter' under the pseudonym 'Gouli-Gouli' between the years 1898 and 1901. Her pieces were mostly satirical observations of colonial life and women's fashion, and attracted some disdain from her literary contemporaries. Described by the colonial writer Alfred Buchanan as belonging to the 'flippant

[3] Ibid.

[4] Nancy Phelan, *The Romantic Lives of Louise Mack* (St Lucia: University of Queensland Press, 1991), p. 30.

school' of journalism, her work was criticised for being deriva-
tive of earlier satirical female writing.[5] Buchanan would go on
to describe Mack – and other female satirists writing for the
Bulletin – as being 'as fond of a varnish of cynicism on
their social writings as certain of their sisters are of a
suggestion of rouge on their faces'.[6] Rebuffed by the literary
elite, the genre for which Mack is remembered is that of romance, a genre described by Buchanan as 'mainly the preserve
and playground of women'.[7]

During her forty-year literary career, Mack wrote sixteen
novels – her final novel, *Maiden's Prayer*, was published the year
before her death in 1935 – as well as a collection of poetry, and
an autobiographical account of the time she spent in the Great
War, which she published in 1915. She was the first female war
correspondent for the *Evening News* and the *Daily Mail*, cov-
ertly documenting the occupation of Antwerp while disguised
as a maid for German soldiers. Despite the serious subject
matter of these pieces, Mack's reputation was not altered by her
wartime writings, and she remained in the Australian public's
imaginary as a writer of romance and serials. This reputation
was only bolstered by the bohemian lifestyle for which she
became renowned. Married, divorced, and remarried – her
second husband being a healthy twenty-one years her junior –
Mack arrived in London in 1901, having left her first husband,
John Percy Creed, a barrister from Dublin whom she married
in 1896. In London she wrote prolifically for Harmsworth Press
and Mills and Boon; she composed *An Australian Girl in London* from an attic room in a boarding house, weak with hunger

---

[5]   Alfred Buchanan, *The Real Australia* (London: T. Fisher Unwin, 1907),
      pp.107-08.

[6]   Ibid.

[7]   Ibid.

and fatigue. She continued to publish as both Louise Mack and Mrs J. P. Creed until 1924 when she married New Zealand Anzac Captain Allen Leyland. Described by her niece, Nancy Phelan, as 'a mass of contradictions', Mack is remembered for her idiosyncratic lifestyle, being 'consistent only in her love of beauty and her ambition to write'.[8]

An Australian Girl in London self-consciously attaches itself to a local tradition of writing on the figure of the Australian Girl. Inaugurated by authors such as Rosa Praed and Ada Cambridge, and crystallised by Catherine Martin's *An Australian Girl* (1890), a classic turn-of-the-century ideal of the Australian Girl is also found in Ethel Castilla's poem of the same name, first published in 1887 and then reprinted with the more definitive title 'The Australian Girl' in 1888. Castilla describes the Australian Girl as energetic yet feminine, and youthful yet wise. She is not submissive to the older traditions of Britain: 'Her frank, clear eyes bespeak a mind', Castilla writes, 'Old-world traditions fail to bind'.[9] But she doesn't stand for radically new traditions either. Rather, she is 'simply self-possessed': carving out a space of her own in relation to the Old and the New Worlds she simultaneously inhabits. In other words, the Australian Girl is a contradictory, paradoxically placed figure, acting as a symbol of independence but also of comparison. Like Australia itself, the Australian Girl is caught between her own singularity and the inevitable comparison with her British sisters: she is uniquely beautiful, yet understood in relation to her Old World counterparts; she is 'kissed' by the hot southern sun, yet strangely 'paler' than the English belles.[10] Moving from Australia to Britain, each

---

[8] Phelan, *The Romantic Lives of Louise Mack*, p. 24.

[9] Ethel Castilla, *The Australian Girl and Other Verses* (Melbourne: George Robertson, 1900), p. 3.

[10] Ibid., p. 2.

Australian Girl takes her enthusiasm for change back to the Old World, confronting the issue of what is worth preserving – and what is worth changing. 'Are we a naturally giddy and pleasure-loving country, I wonder?' asks Sylvia in *An Australian Girl in London*; 'The gaiety and verve we put into our accounts of things, as we tell them to each other, is lacking in this frostbitten island'. For her Australian audience, Mack's heroine traces the expected path of the Australian Girl abroad, her disposition inseparable from the youth of a vigorous and impulsive nation.

At the turn of the twentieth century, Australia was being promoted as 'the land of sunshine and gold' and both the nation and its Australian Girl were rendered through their relations to 'frostbitten' Britain.[11] In *To Try Her Fortune in London: Australian Women, Colonialism, and Modernity* (2001), Angela Woollacott notes that the 'preferred comparison' to the Australian Girl and 'the one most often invoked' was the English Girl.[12] The former was generally cast in a healthier, more positive light by Australian writers around this time. Woollacott comments on a near-contemporary of Mack's, Alice Grant Rosman, who left Australia for London in 1911 and also wrote for Mills and Boon. Rosman regarded the Australian Girl as 'more tenacious, intelligent, useful, practical and energetic' than her English sisters.[13] Rosman is one of many of Mack's contemporaries who travelled to Britain; others include the writers Rosa Praed, Mary Gaunt and Miles Franklin. According to Woollacott, it was not only novelists who tracked this 'Well Worn Path'; singers Nellie Melba and Ada Crossley, and actress Alice Crawford, similarly

[11] *British-Australasian*, 3 March 1898, p. 501.

[12] Angela Woollacott, *To Try Her Fortune in London: Australian Women, Colonialism, and Modernity* (Oxford: Oxford University Press, 2001), p.158.

[13] Ibid. Woollacott is quoting from Rosman's 1913 series, 'Girls Who are Going to London Town'.

helped shape the imagined mobility of the Australian Girl.[14] The Australian Girl is caught between two different, even opposite, conditions, evident even before she goes abroad. Ken Gelder and Rachael Weaver describe the Australian Girl as 'identified through her capacity to move . . . back and forth between "wilderness" . . . and its opposite, cultivation (the garden, the orchard, etc)'.[15] They highlight that she is 'strengthened by the former, but "civilised" through the latter' and suggest that it is 'the combination of these two things' that 'determined the Australian girl's romantic trajectory and where it took her'.[16]

Mack's *An Australian Girl in London* is framed by the exotic and expansive Australian bush in chapter one, and the melancholy albeit lively London boarding house in the final chapters. Sylvia spends much of the novel dreaming about her homeland, lauding Australia by comparison to her European surroundings. She recalls the first moments after boarding the ship to London, 'out into the darkness, the red lights of the coast fading, fading, Australia receding, my eyes brimming, my heart crying "Australia, Australia, I'll never love anyone but you"'. But despite her evident devotion to Australia, Sylvia is aware of 'the mercurial manner of our countrywomen' and says 'goodbye with a heart full of London'. She oscillates between her desire to indulge in her Australian identity and an overwhelming nostalgic loyalty to Britain: before she has even left Australia she signs her first letter as 'Miss Sylvia Leighton, London'. Eventually she begins signing her letters as 'Silver', gesturing to a sense of inferiority she feels as 'only an Australian', especially when read in comparison to the 'moments of pure gold' she experiences as an expatriate.

[14] Ibid., p. 160.

[15] Ken Gelder and Rachael Weaver, *Colonial Australian Fiction: Character Types, Social Formations, and the Colonial Economy* (Sydney: Sydney University Press, 2017), p. 122.

[16] Ibid.

Finally Sylvia becomes 'your little, littlest Silver'; as she fulfils her promise of marriage, she becomes the smallest version of herself. This Australian Girl performs the requirements of romantic narrative in a post-Federation Australia, drawing on her New World charm to revive a tired, antiquated British Empire. However, in order to fulfil her promise of marriage, Sylvia must compromise her strength and her stature, becoming doubly inferior as both the 'littlest' and 'Silver'.

In contrast, fellow Australian Girl in London Emmie Jones, with whom Sylvia develops a very close bond, is 'breaking [her] heart to go back' to Australia. Emmie is an aspiring singer who has embarked on the same journey as Sylvia, believing that 'to get to London is all that is needed to make [one] famous'. Following the trajectory of Nellie Melba, who debuted in London in 1888, Emmie is thrust into 'the battle with the agents' and an 'endless succession of rebuffs, disappointments, chilling receptions' once she completes her studies and embarks on a singing career. Rejection makes her imagine that she will be 'the bitter example' of failure to those back home, complaining that 'Australia should have been big enough for me.' Emmie's singing voice, although 'haunting' and 'soulful', is said to be cold, and Sylvia believes her friend needs her heart broken in order to attain the voice that will make her successful. Emmie fantasises about a young Swedish man, but when he leaves London it fuels her complicated longing for Australia; she 'goes out into Hyde Park, that looks like paddocks in the early morning, and lies on the grass under the plane trees, and crumples up a gum leaf.' Sylvia explains, 'This is not homesickness. If Emmie could go home now she would not. Her roots have taken here.' This predicament both fragments Emmie and strengthens her: although she remains unmarried and homesick, her experience works to transform her voice until she is 'magnificent', ultimately becoming a better singer for it.

Sylvia's journey to London is also a journey through the British Empire, a voyage on a steamship that she describes as a 'miniature white world'. But when the ship stops briefly in British occupied Ceylon, now Sri Lanka, aspects of her own white settler racism become apparent. Sylvia is conscious of her place in what she calls the 'great Imperial scheme'; her romantic choices, for example, remain tied to her Australian and English circles. Imperialism shapes the identity of the Australian Girl, whether she travels along the route of Empire to London or – if one thinks of J.D. Hennessey's *An Australian Bush Track* (1896), also republished in this series – heads into the Australian interior towards the colonial frontier. Sylvia's excitability when she arrives at her destination ('London, London, London, London, *London!*') is endearing, but is the result of a structure that determines where she goes, who she considers for marriage, and how she views herself in relation to the Empire's other people and places.

In this post-Federation narrative, Mack identifies the impossibility of there being only 'an' Australian Girl to which all of the promise of a new nation might be attributed. For Mack, one lone girl cannot sustain all the unrealistic expectations Castilla's centennial poem had placed upon her. Like Australia itself, negotiating its own sense of unification and fragmentation, the Australian Girl is thus always herself and her other at the same time, at once Australian and British, in love and alone, local, expatriated, ambitious and homesick. *An Australian Girl in London* is not a novel about 'the' Australian heroine we might expect, but rather about two Australian Girls, Sylvia and Emmie, each coming to terms with the unique expectations placed upon them by an emerging nation.

SARAH POPE is completing her PhD in Australian Literature at the University of New South Wales.

WORKS CITED

Buchanan, Arthur, *The Real Australia*. London: T. Fisher Unwin, 1907.

Castilla, Ethel, *The Australian Girl and Other Verses*. Melbourne: George Robertson & Co., 1900.

Gelder, Ken and Weaver, Rachael, *Colonial Australian Fiction: Character Types, Social Formations, and the Colonial Economy*. Sydney: Sydney University Press, 2017.

Phelan, Nancy, *The Romantic Lives of Louise Mack*. St Lucia: The University of Queensland, 1991.

Woollacott, Angela, *To Try Her Fortune in London: Australian Women, Colonialism, and Modernity*. New York: Oxford University Press, 2001.

A NOTE ON THE TEXT

This edition of *An Australian Girl in London* follows the first edition of the novel, published (under the author's name 'Mrs. J.P. Creed') in London by T. Fisher Unwin in 1902. The novel went into Unwin's Colonial Library, alongside Rosa Praed's *My Australian Girlhood: Sketches and Impressions of Bush Life* (1902) and a selection of other works of colonial fiction.

Mack had wanted to title her novel *Winter Traces*, but Nancy Phelan notes that the publishers thought *An Australian Girl in London* was 'more ordinary and easy to identify'.

Certain passages in this novel are used by Mack in her later novels, *The Romance of a Woman of Thirty* (1911), *Attraction* (1913). 'Leighton' – the family name given to the novel's heroine Sylvia – is also the name of the family in Mack's early novel, *Teens: A Story of Australian School Girls* (1897) and the sequel, *Teens Triumphant* (1933). The heroine of these novels, Lennie Leighton, is a writer, and the name of her book in Teens Triumphant is *Winter Traces*.

The character introduced as 'Estrella Hawkins' in chapter twelve is sometimes referred to as 'Elfreda'. This has not been altered, in recognition of the strained circumstances under which Mack completed this novel.

The editors of the present text have sought to balance scholarly accuracy with readability. Some punctuation, capitalisation, spelling and hyphenation has been changed for the sake of consistency (e.g. 'Music' to 'music'). Scholars seeking an unamended text of this edition should contact info@grattanstreetpress.com for details.

An Australian Girl
in London

To Lord Beauchamp, late governor of New South Wales, this little book is offered – a slight tribute to deep kindness and sympathy extended towards my fellow-workers, so far away over seas.

LOUISE CREED.

London 1902.

CHAPTER I

Coolloolloo, *April* 190—.

My dear people,

Last night I went down into the Bush to say goodbye.

It was silent – quite silent. It would give me no message. It wrapped up its meaning and withheld it. And the gums, who have always been my friends, were all quiet and a little sullen.

I knew the reason. I read it in their faces. They thought I had rushed to them to say goodbye with a heart full of London.

They knew I had been sitting over the writing table in Cousin Alfred's den writing,

Miss Sylvia Leighton,

London,

for the last half-hour.

They knew I brought them a mind full of excitement and other places. I threw myself down at their feet, and lay with my face against their white kid trunks, smooth as gloves. But in vain. They would have nothing to do with me. They refused to be at one with me though we have so often been one before. I was going away from them, and they were hurt.

So my last hour in the Bush was not the deep hour when the mystery of the great silence got down into my bones, ran up and down my back, and made me feel that Heaven *has* to be. It was just a hurried hour, full of petti-coats, and blouses, and boxes, crossed with wonders at the thought of Naples, Rome, Colombo, spoiled with wander-ing thoughts leaping here and there all over the world I am going around so soon. And the Bush wouldn't have that. I should *think* not.

London! I see it every night. I have been there hun-dreds of times already.

I see a great impossible mass, and grey smoke, smoke, smoke. What I see is so large that it would probably cover all England. But then London *is* large. There's nothing in the world as large as London – to an Australian.

And this great grey mass is all inextricably mixed; the streets are twisted and never-ending. I shall *never* be able to go outside the door without someone to show me the way. And it's partly beautiful, and partly fearful. It makes me feel afraid. *London! To be in London!* Ugh! I would be fright-ened, only that I don't believe I can possibly ever get there.

It is too wonderful.

It is just a week today since it was settled that I should go with Cousin Alfred and Jean to London to have some music lessons, and already I have been to London again and again and again.

I have been so often that I am even a little tired. I feel I know it nearly all. Thinking of it so hard, night and day, picturing, imagining, bringing it suddenly near me, has actually caused me to exhaust London. I have picked the heart out of it. I am a bit tired of it. I have seen it all. I have thought of it so hard that I've transported myself there, and

run through it sixty times as quickly as a Cook's tourist.[1]
Isn't that funny? That's where the curse of a vivid imagination comes in. It tells you all about a place before you
get there. That's why Shakespeare never travelled. Home
tomorrow. And then two weeks. And then——

SYLVIA LEIGHTON, LONDON.

---

[1] Thomas Cook & Son of London published their first *Cook's Handbook for London* in 1877; it was a series that lasted well into the twentieth century and extended to other places around the world.

CHAPTER II

Written at Sea.

Dear everybody,

'Begin from the minute you left,' said Peggy.

But I won't. I'll skip two hours, during which we had lunch. I settled our cabins up a little. Then came the great fixing up of deckchairs. People moved round and settled definitely the places of hundreds of cane chairs, cane lounges, canvas chairs, little children's chairs. This was a most important affair, and took up half an hour. Then I'll tell you how Jean and I walked up and down the deck, and privately investigated the people walking up and down past us. We both came to the conclusion we had never seen so many plain, homely, uninteresting people in our lives.

Two hours after leaving those dear old steady Heads is a time when most people *do* look plain, homely and uninteresting, I imagine. We never thought of it that way. We just decided that out of hundreds and hundreds of passengers there was not one man or woman who had the faintest attraction for us. None of the girls were pretty. All the married women were common-looking. All the men looked stupid. They all had such bad complexions, such small eyes.

'I couldn't make friends with anybody,' said Jean.

'Neither could I,' said I.

'I'm glad you're here,' said Jean.

'I'm glad *you're* here,' said I.

In fact they were all frights. I daresay we were worse than any of them, in their eyes. There is nothing like the first hours at sea to bring out all the latent antagonism of man to man. I am sure we all hated each other, if the truth would out. Such a thing as a sunny smile was not to be had for love or money.

But that's all over now.

We have left Adelaide. We have left Fremantle. We are away in the Indian Ocean. The dreaded Great Australian Bight was as smooth as glass, as blue as a turquoise. We have said goodbye to Australia. Ah, dear country, I'll never love any place as I love you. That's a promise. Hold me to it till I die.

And now the ship is settling down. We are going to be sociable. Little men with big heads are running about on thin legs with pieces of paper in their hands, asking people to come to meetings and go on committees. Poor little men! What would ships do without them? But I suppose there never was a ship without them. They constitute part of the voyage.

Heavens! The sort of people that travel! What a disillusionment!

I cherished a secret idea that I would meet all kinds of delightful, charming, cultured people on a long sea voyage, and we'd talk about Shelley, and Rossetti, and Chopin, and Italy, and Greece, and Paris. Or they would talk and I would listen. There would be moonlight thrown in, and a great stillness broken only by the murmuring of the waves.

But no!

And, of course! Those people are the poor things who have too much soul to make a fortune. They who travel from Australia are the money makers, the businesspeople – butchers, and bakers, and ironmongers – people who don't waste time looking for the unseen, but convert the visible into gold or silver as quickly as possible. Strange that I never thought of that till I came to sea.

Nothing can give one a more forceful, I might even say lurid, impression of the follies that go to make us men and women than a long sea voyage. There you see people without disguise. They have no sheltering home of their own to disappear into till their ugliness is forgotten a little, nor have we. No one has the advantage of being able to drape himself or herself with the little things of life that act as drapes and flouncings, such as big houses and little houses, friends and relatives, and the nice things every-one knows about one that here have to be learned anew by everyone.

When you have seen three hundred women unveiled in this way you cannot help but shudder – not at them, but at yourself for being like them. They all have the same tricks. So have you, and you never knew they were tricks till you saw them displayed *en masse* hour after hour.

They all turn up their eyes in the same way. They all tell the same lies. They all repeat the same superficial observation as if they meant it. They all ask silly questions about each other's health. 'How are you this morning?' 'How are you today?' They all don't care a bit about the answers. They all do this, and they all do that, affected theatrical little things. Harmless indeed; but when repeated again and again their significance leaps out at you, and the horrible decadence of modern people makes you distrust yourself and everyone else. When these things are presented to you, not singly – yourself, the actress – and not in threes or fours – your friends, the performers – but in scores, and fifties, and hundreds, daily, hourly, on every occasion, you see through your sex, you see through the race, and you understand how few indeed are the single-minded, the sincere, and you can never again have the same old trust in people whom you had no reason to distrust.

So much for the people.

But the journey, the journey! Oh, why has it never been put into song or story? It became a joy the day we left Adelaide. All the waves went out of the sea, and our ship marched on and marched on, day after day, night after night, through the warm, still ocean. I sat for hours gazing at that great shining reach all round me, but though I grew to know it well, so that it never could be forgotten or mis-understood again, I could not satisfy myself with a parallel beautiful and true enough.

One day the real thing flashed across me – like frozen castor oil!

After that I gave up looking for similes and accepted things as they were.

Ah, well! The Indian Ocean has taught me the mock-ery of living on land and thinking you know the meaning of blues and greens. As if anyone could know even half the blue in the world who had never lived a month on water. Hour after hour I sit on deck without weariness, watching that great flood passing under my eyes. It lies so still, day after day, week after week, that I can't believe it is the sea. Yet ever its colour changes. Today it shines like a polished floor built of a single turquoise. Tomorrow, thick and deep, it lies over the face of the earth, like millions of melted sapphires. The creamy pink on our ship's side is reflected on the polished surface; it turns a pale, moving violet there as we pass along. Then there are days when someone seems to have poured down a seaful of blue-green oil, so bright, so heavy, so deeply coloured, that you feel as if you could cut with a knife the *colour* alone. Then there are other days when all the thickness and solidity go out of it, and it lies like a pale blue fragile sky dropped from Heaven for us to voyage over.

And the sunsets!

I have learned a sky secret. The setting steals its meaning from the lands over which it sets. As we move along, the sunsets change with the rest of the world.

As we come near Egypt they take on sharp outlines and burning colours. Night after night the breathless end of day in the tropics sees the ocean turn blood-red under an immense sky as scarlet as hell, and swept with wild greens and burning yellows. The sea seems to set as well as the sky.

But as we steal towards Italy the sky will grow soft and tender. One great kind wash of rose will sweep the sun plains, and over it will hover simple white clouds. We have come to the place of watercolour sunsets that stir the breast dimly, like sweet, faint music away in the distance.

The most beautiful part of it all is that the most beautiful is always to come – remembrance hoarded away in the future, waiting for us, till the present becomes past, and the joy of these lovely days, now so near, recedes, and we can look back, and look, and look, and call up days stored with golden moments, when there was no veil between us and the beauty of the world.

~

On and on for twelve long days, across the Indian Ocean. Through the Tropic of Capricorn, across the Equator, from Fremantle to Ceylon.

The earth world fades away, life begins and ends with the doings on board this miniature white world, the *Omrac*.

To this famous colonial politician in white duck clothes, to pick up all the potatoes and get back with them to the bucket before anyone else in the potato race is of far greater importance than to secure Mr Chamberlain's assistance in his great Imperial scheme.[2] The scheme is the concentration of a lifetime. The potatoes are only the potatoes of an hour. But the potatoes knock the scheme to smithereens, and turn the politician into a cross little boy when that old man with the grey moustache from New Zealand slips the last potato into the bucket and wins the race.

All round us gleam sunny sky and sunny sea. The earth has disappeared. It never was. It never will be again.

That is merely a specimen of the chaotic way in which one thinks at sea. You have heard of sea legs in contra-distinction to land legs. There are also sea brains. Their chief characteristic is slipperiness. Everything slides off them. The books we read, the thoughts we think, all drop

---

[2] Joseph Chamberlain was Secretary of State for the Colonies from 1895 to 1903; during this time he proposed the creation of an Imperial Council to unite the colonies and strengthen the British Empire.

helplessly to the deck, and lie about there in dull, but not unhappy, confusion.

And what does it matter? The sea is the King of Lotus Eaters, and we are in his land today. Who is foolish enough to want to be keen, to desire to think clear, deep, penetrating thoughts, to bother about the thoughts of other people put into books with labour?

I watch the sea wash the earthiness out of these hundreds of people. It sweeps away their scheming plots and plans. It turns them back towards their childhood. Ah, if it had them long enough it would make them all as lovely at heart as its great, simple, unscheming self.

But that cannot be. And in the interval, while the sea wipes out their earth-life, and they are in the transition stage, they alternate between simple, happy children and restless beings robbed of their acquired heritage of plot and plan, their search for money, and struggle for fame.

All day long we do nothing. And yet there is never an unoccupied moment. The days are filled to the brim. We often go to bed tired out. Perhaps the fatigue springs from these hundreds of individualities pressing so closely and continuously on us. All day they are with us, and all night. We can never get away from them. The ego aches as if it were in a cramped sardine box. It wants to go off by itself sometimes, in the queer way egos have. But the sardine box holds it tight. All it can do is kick a little at the lid.

What do we do all day?

The First Class, which always represents fashion, gives a ball, and doesn't invite the Second Class. The Second Class, which invariably represents intellect, gives a party, and hangs up the notice of it in Greek.

The First Class doesn't know Greek. It comes, and looks at the notice, and goes away baffled.

In the daytime the great white decks are surrounded with nets. There we play our games. The hours are mapped out with never-ending pastimes. The programmes hang at the top of the hatchway.

At ten o'clock, ladies play off deck billiards; meeting of fancy dress ball committee in saloon; bottle-driving tournament begins. At eleven, meeting of committee to arrange children's maypole dance; rehearsal of 'Sunset'; the second Calcutta sweep to be drawn. At twelve, the Hon. John Jones and Sir Peter Squail, Met. C., play off their dead heat in throwing the sand-bag.

And perhaps at twelve-thirty there is a funeral in the steerage. The purser is reading the burial service. The ship grows suddenly quiet. Her motion is slowed. Many passengers go to look over into the steerage. Many others turn away and bury themselves in books. A few weep.

A door high up in the ship's side is opened. Something wrapped in brown canvas is thrown out. It drops down, down, into the waves. And we have passed on. Already it is half a mile behind.

For an hour a shadow is cast over the ship. Who was he? An old man. What did he die of? Heart disease. Was he alone? Quite alone, going home to his son in Ireland. Then the gloom lifts and life goes on again as usual. It seems a little less important, that is all. That brown bag tossed to the waves, without hearse or coffin or crape, gives Death a new simplicity.

At two-thirty the Great Ladies' Cricket Match begins – Australia versus New Zealand. Everybody on board tries to get a look. The decks are crowded. Wild 'barracking' goes on. It is a fiercely hot afternoon. To lie on a block of ice would seem far more suitable than to play a cricket match. But the teams are in such deadly earnest that temperature is nothing to them. They all wear white linen frocks and sailor hats. Some are matrons with big families. Some are old maids. Some are young girls. Many of them never threw a ball in their lives before. But – or perhaps I should say *so* – mercy on us, how they throw them now! What excitement prevails! An intercolonial match on land is nothing to this in mid-ocean.

Our elegant cousin Jean is delicious. She throws herself full-length across the deck and stops the balls in her skirts. The *Sea Urchin*, our paper, describes this as 'brilliant fielding'.

The Australian-ism of the ship comes out. The land of cricketers asserts itself. Over the Indian Ocean go wild whoops and huzzas, bursts of clapping, loud spontaneous bravos, and mad cheers and peals of laughter.

There are men crowded about the match who have beaten England on its own wicket, but there isn't a trace of scorn in their eyes as they watch this exhibition of pure feminine heroics. Their blazing red faces are full of the keenest interest. Never in their lives have they beheld cricket like this: where the woman with the longest skirts is the best fielder; where the batswoman blinks and jumps when the ball comes towards her, and looks away to sea as she hits out before her; where the bowler is changed every minute or two; where the umpire is treated with deliberate scorn; where one of the eleven slips out and gets a girl from the 'attendance' to come in and take her place, and then returns and plays herself, and makes her substitute stay on and play also till discovered.

At four o'clock the match is suspended, while the ship goes down to tea. At four-thirty it continues, and lasts till dinner time, when – well, I won't say which side wins. You shall remain as we were – at sea.

And at night – a breathless furnace of a night – the band plays the 'Blue Danube' on the lighted decks, and the old Indian Ocean looks up at our red lights, and sees white shoulders and black figures revolving, and watches, through the portholes, people playing card tournaments in the saloon, and wonders why those strange things don't feel the heat.

We *do* feel it, as a matter of fact. But, by some mysterious accident, we have all been set going and can't stop ourselves.

And besides, nothing matters. To be hot is of as little importance as to be cool. It is easier to play cricket than to refuse to play. Those are the ethics of life at sea.

~

'And we came to the Isle of Palms.'

The twelve days, that seemed like twelve years, are over at last.

It is early, early in the morning when I sit up in my berth and look through my porthole and see a foreign sail cut clear against a misty rose and onyx sky: a tall, brown, curving sail leaning above a low, brown dhow, and in the dhow a black man guiding his craft.

The East! The East! The East! That is my first glimpse of the East! How it thrills! How it stuns! The curved sail, the silent black, the onyx sky are blown with magic. They thrust one into a new world. Yet from the deck, later,

Colombo looks like Sydney seen from Fort Denison, with its gardens gleaming down to the harbour's edge.

Over the waters we go gaily, a party of eight. The rose has left the sky. The harbour of Colombo is black with swarming craft and loud with hundreds of native voices. Our black oarsmen guide us towards that low line of emerald rising out of the waves. Nearer and nearer, till the green trees and the red houses are almost upon us, and we have come to Ceylon.

We land, and stand stunned on the wooden pier.

'You lady! You lady! You lady!'

A deafening babble of voices, a sea of brown faces and turbaned heads. Overhead a blazing sky. We are in the Orient.

Dozens of rickshaw men gather round us. They almost drag us to their vehicles, clamouring, coaxing, beseeching. It is a wonder we don't leave a limb or two among them. We are going to the hotel at the water's edge – the Oriental. It is only a few steps, so we walk, laughing insanely. We all go out of the wooden shed into the scarlet street. We are dazed with many waters, and stand, stunned again, looking along the flat town.

A great, gay note of red rises and comes towards us.

The earth underfoot is red. Against the rose sky, flame trees rear their great, red, leafless flowers. And there are scarlet houses and bazaars all round us.

But all is kept in perfect Oriental harmony by the impression of greenness from coconut trees, the blue sea flowing near, and the scent of heavy flowers.

Life! It seizes and pinions us for a moment, then tosses us to the winds, and says, 'Play, children, play! I made the world as a playground for you, and you would not understand. Now you can see my meaning. Play, play, play!'

Everybody plays.

Old fat men and women, old thin men and women, quiet people, thoughtful people, girls and youths and children and babies, all yield to the mad intoxication of Colombo, and rush here and there, on foot or in rickshaws, laughing, screaming, jabbering all the long day.

The hotels are full of our ship's passengers. We meet them everywhere. At the Oriental we come across them in the cool, bare, stained halls, on the verandahs, in the great, shady dining hall, where barefoot Cingalese[3] go noiselessly about with solemn black eyes, white clothes and white turbans, carrying fragrant Ceylon tea and coffee, dishes of strange fruits, dishes of curries to these glad Australian people who have renewed or deepened their youth in this one day's holiday from the sea.

The first ride in a rickshaw is a tremendous sensation. You feel like a queen. You own the whole world. You have *a man* – a flesh-and-blood man – running in harness between the shafts of your tall, black perambulator with two big wheels, and a hood that goes up and down. Off he tears. His rate is desperately swift. He is so thin that you fear he will break in pieces, that you will be arrested for cruelty to dumb animals. Bones stick out of his shoulders, elbows, knees and feet. He is a very highly polished trotter. His skin catches the sun on it and shines like a looking glass. Through the warm, electric air you dash. Your spirits go up, and up, and up. You try to remember Sydney. How far, far away it seems! Its trams and 'buses and trains and wide, white streets seem to exist only in a

---

[3] Archaic spelling of Sinhalese.

dream. This is the only life you have ever known. In one moment, with one step from a boat to a wharf, you have changed your identity. All responsibilities vanish down the scented street. A great hand seems to slap you back into the primeval gaiety of a simple savage.

All the while we ride, children and women run along beside us in the golden sunlight.

On the red road by the sea a tiny, naked siren rolls her soft black eyes at my left, and tosses her bare arms in attitudes that would madden an artist.

'Gimme pocket money, you nice auntie!' The haunting cadences of her baby voice steal down into the senses. As she has no clothes at all, 'pocket money' is not without humour.

She and other little girls and boys throw big, stalkless purple and yellow flowers into our laps. They cry, 'I gif them you, you my nice *mum*-ma!' We take the flowers. They run along beside us for a quarter of a mile. Then they begin to beg payment. 'You giv me monnee, lady,' wail their plaintive voices.

If you don't, the next act in the comedy sees them try and grab their flowers away from you, and sees you toss them out. Then they pick them off the scarlet road, and dash away towards another rickshaw where some other laughing and enraptured Australian flies along in the same maze of delight as your own.

All day long we rush through the township in rickshaws, through the Cinnamon Gardens, round the lake, out to Mount Lavinia, by that wonderful road along the sea's edge. For seven miles we drive in the shadow of tangled coconuts, banyans, and trees that are strangers to us.

I said to myself as we drove, 'Tiger, tiger, burning bright', and almost expected to see one. How delightful to me would have been the sight of two snapping eyes from that jungle on the right! By the way, it wasn't a jungle at all, but how could I resist calling it so?

Everybody does the same thing. At Mount Lavinia we meet our ship's people in hundreds. Ah, Mount Lavinia! How bittersweet it was to come to you and go away! You scented hill, sloping down to the shimmering Indian Ocean, with a hotel on your summit, and green gardens full of fair women in white frocks drinking tea on the verandahs, or in the shade on the grass, with black men in white suits carrying teas and iced drinks to happy travellers, and a little warm breeze blowing spice and fragrance in their faces – how nice it must be to be you, and to give such pure, wild pleasure to so many thousands of artless, untravelled, unsophisticated people!

Says Alfred, before the sun sets, 'I'm going to buy some presents for the girls. Come along with me.'

Off we tear in a rickshaw each, through the warm, red, crowded, laughing, jangling, flower-scented streets. Alfred is an old traveller. He knows a shop where you can get moonstones that don't drop out and turn into glass an hour after you have paid twenty times as much as they were worth for them. Jean goes along with a crowd of friends to the Galle Face,[4] so I have Alfred to myself. I am rather glad there is nobody else there.

'Now, how muchee you wantee these moonee stones?' begins Alfred. We have entered one of the little shops

---

[4] This is the location of the Victoria Masonic Temple in Colombo on the west coast of Sri Lanka (known as Ceylon during British colonial rule). It opened in September 1901.

near the Hotel Oriental. We seat ourselves at a little table with a little oriental table cover on it, and half-a-dozen solemn men with lovely, pathetic black eyes grouped around us.

'Me welly poor mannee; me givee you fairee thing allee samee.'

'Alfred, they're not Chinamen! Talk plain English to them.'

But such an old traveller as Alfred could not possibly do that.

'Avez-vous des sapphires, and show me your o-pal and let's see your feel-a-gree, feel-a-gree, comprenez?'

So he goes on. Heaven knows which is the more unintelligible, the merchants or Alfred.

While he fights it out with them, and they come gradually – very gradually from twenty pounds to one pound, ten shillings, a dark creature says to me, sweetly, 'I remember you, lady.'

I say I have never been here before, but he isn't abashed.

'You know Sirupert Jimmes?'

'Sir Rupert James?'

'You know Mr 'Ordern.'

'Hordern?'

'You know Lady Dickenson.'

'No.'

'Oh, yes, lady, *you* know Lady Dickenson. You know Sir John Georges.'

I get tired of disowning titled people from my own land, but he pulls out a dirty, filthy packet of cards and hands me one. On it is written in terrific writing, with a little 'r' and a little 'j', 'Sir rupert jambs'; then another, with a very swagger colonial woman's name on it, written in a

Mary-Jane hand that would reduce the owner of the name to pulp.

'Did they give you these?' I ask.

'Yes, lady.'

I laugh out loud and he takes them away hastily. I hope the people represented on those dirty pasteboards may never have the painful shock of seeing *how* they are represented. What masterpieces of fraud they are, those innocent-eyed creatures! Up to every trick on earth. They find out and remember the names of their customers; then they write cards to show other people what a superior connection they have, but they give the other people too little credit for common sense. Probably because they encounter so little of it in their business dealings with travelling colonials.

At last Alfred has bought seven rings, pressed one on me, tied the rest up in his handkerchief, and off we go for a wild race round the town, behind two pairs of twinkling bare black legs.

Here comes a Pause.

While I tell you *never* to show this letter to anyone who has been to Colombo.

If they have been there they will want to forget the temporary insanity that overtook them that yellow breeze-blown day when they rushed through the scented scarlet city among the palm trees, from morn till dewy eve, buying, bargaining, laughing, screaming, all in a hurry, in a concentrated burst of gaiety, with a fortnight's sea behind and three weeks' sea to come.

All too soon the wonderful day draws to an end. Nothing that may come later can raise the same ineffable happiness as this first foreign port. Only one day, but to many people it will become a golden memory that will never cease to glitter a little through the humdrum of their lives when they 'settle down' again.

Sunset finds us at the Galle Face, that great, gleaming, white hotel at the far end of the yellow sea beach. The moon comes out. The coconut trees wave in the sea breeze. The Indian Ocean turns silver. A mile away, the lights of Colombo gleam redly.

We dine at a little table in the window, looking out through palm trees over the shining sea.

The great hall is full of chatter and laughter. The excitement of the early morning has deepened gradually all day. It is at its height now. None of these women in their crushed white frocks and white straw hats, these men in grey slouch hats and thin suits, ever had a trouble in their lives. They have always lived here. Every night they have dined in this high white room with its many windows looking seawards, its lights, its bright fruit on the great stand in the centre, its black-bearded waiters stealing noiselessly about on bare feet.

Then comes coffee on the verandahs, or out on the little green tables in the moonlight under the flickering coconut trees.

The Cingalese merchants grow very urgent now. They have stalls in the hotel, little shops here and there all over the place. They *must* sell. We shall all be gone soon. Their prices begin to come down. Down, down, down, down, *down*.

And even further down.

In the morning this filigree necklet was thirty-five shillings. After lunch it came down to twenty-five. After dinner it leapt from twenty to fifteen. Jean said, to get rid of the man, 'Two shillings.'

'Oh, lady, 'ow can you?' said he. But down, down it came. From fifteen to twelve, twelve to ten, ten to five. And at last he thrust it into her hand and said, 'Then you take it, lady, two shillings.' And then Jean had the brazenness to say she didn't want it.

At eleven o'clock, everyone – in a penniless condition – gets back to the big ship in the stream. What a monster she seems! What an enemy! How we hate the thought of returning again, screwing ourselves up, and resuming all the cramped conditions of life on a crowded liner.

But it has to be done. At twelve we move slowly, slowly. Ceylon recedes. The magic day is over.

Next morning a ship laden with moonstone brooches, filigree ornaments, ivory elephants, toy rickshaws, half-pounds of Ceylon tea, clean clothes washed in the lake at Colombo, and sunburnt, worn-out Australians ploughs away towards her next landing place – Ismailia. On board is a bewildered girl, whom you will know by the name of Sylvia, but who doesn't know herself at all.

~

The passengers begin to grow more clear-cut as the days go. One by one they stand out from the heterogeneous mass of men and women who all look so marvellously alike at first.

The doctor is a person of interest. He is a thin, old, long-legged man in navy blue, with a white moustache, a little blue cap, and a long straight back. Twenty years he has been in the service. Can he have any illusions left? As we talk together I scan him over carefully, looking for illusions. Indeed, he has a few still. He still admires a pretty woman. He still finds children lovable little objects. He still sees the humour of life.

'How do you like Sydney, doctor?'

'Oh, jolly little place, awfully jolly little place. When there, I spend most of my time up in your Blue Mountains. I run up to Katoomba as soon as I leave the ship. Tell truth, my friends in Sydney have a way of getting up picnics for me and that sort of thing, don't you know? Or I go to dinner, and after dinner they take me out in a little boat, and I have to tuck up my trousers and the water comes in. A great treat to me, don't you know, after twenty years on water, to be taken out in a little boat, and tuck up my trousers, and be rowed about the harbour.'

One hot, airless night in Capricorn he strolls up as I lean over the bulwarks. The moonlight falls on his old red face and kind old eyes.

'Fond of poetry?'

'That depends.'

'Do you know "The Lost Drink"?'

His eyes twinkle in the moonlight. Two or three girls gather round us. He looks at us with a half-funny, half-melancholy look, and begins a parody on 'The Lost Chord'. It tells of a man who got a drink once – a wonderful drink. He never could get another like it. All his life he searched for the man who mixed it for him. And so on. And so on. Until he is left with the hope that on the other shore he will find that drink once more. Poor old doctor! Is there a reason, hidden beneath his kindly gaiety, that gives that song a peculiar meaning to him? The ship says he looks upon the wine when it is red – I suppose most ship doctors do. And the pathos of the recitation – or is it bathos? – does not die away from my mind for a long time.

Ah me! What a mixture we all are!

Mr Bowles is a plump young Australian in white flannels, who always says 'Hearts *is*' when trumps are turned up at whist. Can anyone help detesting a man in white flannels who says 'Hearts is'?

Then there are three sunburnt tea-planters from Ceylon – Mr Wigram, Mr O'Donnell and Mr Hobson, Scotchman, Irishman and Englishman – all coming home to see their 'maters', all bachelors, and all suffering a recovery from a series of farewelling in Colombo. A passenger asks Mr Wigram to write in her autograph book one night. She is a lady who has loudly commented on the disgraceful condition of Those Men From Ceylon, who – and to be quite just – are really *only* suffering a recovery. I saw the three of them stealing out of the saloon with the book in their hands. Later on Mr Wigram comes back and gives it to its owner. His line of poetry is:

'The stag at eve had drunk its fill.'

And the writing matches the sentiment. It doesn't look in the least sober.

It is in the third week of the journey that the unloveliness of the human race becomes most apparent. Is there no such thing as a nice man or a charming woman? When are we most ourselves? At sea or on land?

That is a problem I shall never be sure of.

The only persons who appear to advantage by this time are the misanthropes, who have had nothing to do with anyone. They have been here before. It is always an old traveller who begins by keeping aloof, and ends by being the one anyone still wants to know.

Next time I travel I'm going to be a misanthrope like Alfred. He won't have anything to do with anyone, unless aged under eight. He sits in his deckchair, reads, refuses to go to committee meetings, refuses to put the tail on the pig, refuses to chase potatoes in the tropics, refuses to play in euchre tournaments, to sing at concerts, to get himself up for the fancy dress ball, refuses all the allurements of social life at sea, and just reads and smokes, and walks the deck, and plays deck billiards with an old man who is nearly stone-deaf. 'This is the way to travel,' says Alfred, when we grumble at the people whom we have always with us.

Did anybody ever say the earth would be all right only for the well-meaning people, or has it been left to me? I won't shirk the task. I'll say it loud and long.

I took to getting up early. I had my bath overnight, and was up on deck before the sun. All in vain. Always there was a woman coming towards me, and always on the tip of her tongue was a remark, and always my bringing-up saved *her* if it nearly killed me.

'Good morning. You're up early too!'

'Good morning. Yes.'

'Isn't it lovely?'

'Yes.'

'I do think it's so *lovely*.'

'Yes.'

'We ought to be getting our early tea soon.'

'Yes.'

Then another well-meaning woman would join us, and 'Good morning. You're up early too! Isn't it *lovely*?' would follow, and presently they would reach the tea. By that time there would be a crowd round us, and the exquisite early air, flushed still with rose, would be filled with 'Good-morning-you're-up-early-toos' and 'Isn't-it-lovelys?' till all hope of merging into the morning's lovely mystery was lost forever.

Another ship remark is, 'Isn't it hot?' The answer to which is, 'Oh, *isn't* it!'

But funnier than anything else is this. Every time these hundreds of women pass each other, in the saloon, in the passages, on the stairs, on the decks, they *smile*. Into that smile, they wildly try to put something – some deep, deep meaning, some message, and as they have no message, no meaning, their effort is in vain. Yet they never pass each other without it. Soon it becomes worn to shreds. Soon it is a mere pained pressing back of the lips, or a hollow enlargement of the eye. *Very* soon you learn to dread it as you see it coming towards you. You would do anything to dodge it. You go along the other side of the table if you have to meet it near. You try to pass it blankly, but your lips twitch in spite of yourself. In dozens, in hundreds, it is shot at you and everyone else all day long. As everyone passes everyone, everyone smiles. The ship is full of smiles. The air is full of smiles. Even the calm, wise sea is riddled with smile-shot.

Now I know why men grow beards.

But we were passing through the worst of the tropics! So much must be forgiven us all.

Day after day we wake, cold with heat moisture touched by the warm air. We get up more dead than alive. In the cramped space of our cabins we totter about wearily, looking for our clothes. We drag ourselves round to the baths, we float in cold saltwater as long as the stewardess will leave us. Then comes the purgatory of dressing. It is only half past seven, but the cabin is worse than an oven. Every movement is an effort. Slowly we begin to dress. Our faces, and necks, and arms, and hands drip, drip, drip. Before we have got into our white blouses we are almost worn out, melted away. It would kill us to put on collars. Powder is an absolute necessity; never travel without it. We powder our arms and throats, our hands and faces. We turn our necks down and down, further every day, until at last the whole ship comes to breakfast in an almost *décolleté* state. Even a thin chain round the neck is too much to be endured.

Breakfast – melting stewards in white clothes, white shoes, and blazing red faces. The little brown shutters are over all the portholes on the sunny side of the saloon. In the yellowy-brown light all the women look ghastly.

We crawl up on deck and flop into our chairs. The heat grows heavier, clammier. The sky is a yellowy-grey, like smoke over fire. At eleven the stewards bring us ices on deck. By one we are nearly dead.

All day long the melting continues. Stout people begin to look thinner. Thin people are like ghosts.

Day after day, day after day, we steadily melt away.

And all night too.

All the stewards are going to leave at the end of the voyage. They are always, on every voyage, in the tropics. Half the passengers sleep up on deck. Others creep into the dining saloon when night is well on, and lie on the floor, or on the divans against the walls. They are waked at half past four by stewards beginning the day's scrubbing and sweeping. What a strange, weird time it is! I think everyone goes a little 'dotty'.

To sit still for fourteen days in a deckchair, and find your hands and face slowly melting off you, gives you a queer feeling, as if this isn't the world at all.

Round the corner is the doctor's cabin.

Everyone is dying and goes to him now. He treats everyone alike – a big black pill. He has been through the tropics how many scores of times? He knows what doesn't kill.

'Isn't this Hell, doctor?' said one woman.

'Hell! There's only one devil in Hell!'

Oh, my gracious, what a time! Only two things are worth anything on earth – the thin white blouse and the long iced squash.

There are only three indispensable things for women this voyage – powder, white blouses, lemon squashes. Yet all day people are saying ominously, 'Wait till we get to the Red Sea! *Then…*'

And then one day, after the longest time in the whole wide world, we enter the Red Sea. We pass Mocha. Away in the distance we can see the sacred city at the sea's edge, its palms against the sky.

More than the sight is the thrill that goes through this raw Australian breast – of age, antiquity, romance, *coffee* – at the sacred name of Mocha.

And the Red Sea, so dreaded, is a dancing sea blown over with a cool, fresh breeze. The worst is past. Otherwise, this letter never could have been written by your,

NEARLY MELTED SILVER.

CHAPTER III

April 190—.

Dear everyone,

Early, early – one breaking, rose-flushed morning – we creep in from the Red Sea.

The canal holds out its arms to us and we pass through. Away in the distance stretches Suez, a white glimmer across the sapphire waves, a stiff white city lying along the edge of the waters.

Past the blue houses on the left shore, past the grey houses and the white houses; past the gay French hotel, with grassed terrace under the trees, set out alluringly with little chairs and little tables; past vivid, gleaming lines of emerald, dashes of tenderest green, breaking along the canal side, and stealing on our senses the sweet, poignant charm of green trees seen for the first time after days and nights of waves and waters.

And every now and then that great, inimitable, unerring artist, the East, flecks in on the picture a dart of scarlet – a red fez on some copper-coloured brow.

Vermilion – that the impressionist swears by – here is your vermilion for you! But see how this artist uses it;

see how nature understands its value. A dash, a flash, just enough scarlet to thrill without palling. Even as you look it has gone, leaving behind an impression as of jewels seen for a moment only, then withdrawn, which is the true romance and reason for jewels and vermilion alike.

On, on, on. Narrowing banks nearly meet in front of us. The water before us runs on like a lengthening green snake. We creep along, slowly and still more slowly. And Egypt opens out to our wondering, awe-stricken eyes – eyes that reverence as only Australian eyes can reverence.

The desert begins – vast, silent, melancholy, monotonous. It strikes us to the heart. It brings back to us the land behind us, our fair young island continent, glimmering away in the far Pacific. Australia rises up before us. The silence hovers over her plains; she, too, has her melancholy, monotonous reaches. And so the desert, the aged, wrinkled, time-worn desert, sings to us of our own young country.

Away, away, and away. Yellow sand and little black hillocks: away, and away and away to the right and to the left of us.

By the water's edge, bulrushes and palm trees call to us when an Egyptian settlement is approaching. Mud houses and flat roofs, women in dense black, veiled to the eyes, some of them, and Arabs running along the banks with us – brown creatures, copper-coloured creatures, lean-legged beings – shrieking for pennies they never get.

So green is the water at our bow, such pea-green, blue-green, salad-green, that again it looks as if you could cut the *colour* out of it with a knife.

All day the yellowy-grey desert lies under the yellowy-grey sun. In the afternoon, dim purples creep over the grey; the sand is misted with a dull, low note of dusky plum colour.

And the day dies down – dies down. Then sunset – such a sunset! The desert turns into a purple symphony. A purple cloud, rose-washed and fantastic, hovers over a white lagoon. The dull violet deepens in the sand. A deeper amethyst creeps from the shores at the canal's edge.

The sky is a violet garden. But, even as we look, it throws away its violets and breaks into crimson. The lagoon turns gold and rose under the new canopy above.

And the sand waves creep on and on, till they reach the waters of the Nile. In a vast overflow the Nile has swept over its banks and washed miles across the desert. Here, in the sunset, it lies on our left in one huge sheet of fiery water, with little islands of dark reeds and rushes creeping up blackly from its glowing waves.

Behind us comes the slow procession of stately ships following us towards the Mediterranean with a sort of haughty humility, so large and dignified that they suffer silently at the narrowness of this passage of water cut for them by a man's brain through God's earth.

Tennyson's line has its fullest meaning here, in this fading evening at the desert's edge:

The stately ships glide on.[5]

The words come to the lips as the great, silent, human-looking creatures follow one another with a dumb, inimitable grace, shooting silver searchlights over the waters, and lighting up the ships that move in front of the solemn procession.

[5] From Alfred Lord Tennyson's 'Break, Break, Break', in *Poems* (1842). The correct line is: 'And the stately ships go on… '.

And then darkness, Egyptian darkness, and midnight, and Port Said, and the Arabs coaling under our porthole, making a picture for us of magnificent composition, so full of life, pose, action, grace – so perfect in its shape and form and colour, with red cressets[6] blazing at each edge of the dense black coal-dredge, the black dust rising, the dark figures showing redly against the coal's deep blackness, the lights of Said glimmering across the water – a picture so superb that it seems to me to be calling aloud to some great master, 'Come, come and paint me. All I wait for is the master hand to catch me on canvas and to hand me down to the future.' Harry Race, a young artist, comes and calls me loudly at my door. 'Don't miss the finest thing you ever saw in your life,' he cries. I wake up, get into clothes, and rush on to the first saloon deck. Two o'clock: Jean hasn't been to bed at all. We hang over and watch. There's Port Said, a stone's throw away – wicked, diabolical, enticing Port Said.

We can't land – smallpox. The night wind sweeps over the city lying there as if tired of its wickedness.

We eat figs and Turkish Delight, and go to bed before dawn, too tired to watch a minute longer. The day in the canal wears one to a fraction; I don't quite know why.

SYLVIA.

---

[6] A metal dish of oil that is set alight and usually attached to a long pole.

CHAPTER IV

OFF THE BALEARIC ISLANDS, *May* 190–.

DEAR PEGGIE,

This letter is *particularly* addressed to you. First, because it is all about a romantic adventure. Second, because you've never had one, my poor old romancing Peg.

Jean and I loitered late in Naples. Alfred went back early. We begged an hour longer, an hour more of that sweet, lingering twilight over the blue bay, an hour more of that enticing arcade, those black-eyed women with their thick dark hair dressed so cunningly, parted on one side, puffed out above the forehead, and rolled on top in a thick coil – stiff with dirt, it may be, for the dirt in Naples is like no other dirt, surely. They linger in it and love it so, the awful, indescribable smell that haunts every street and is to be met out on the way to Bagnoli, driving round the bay with its fringe of villas and oleander gardens, everywhere in and out of Naples.

We had tea at the Hotel Bristol, out on the roof in an amethyst sunset. The light misled us. We lingered and lingered till time grew short. Then we took a cab hastily and directed the hideous old driver to take us to the boat, *le vaisseau*, steamer, ship.

He made a strange noise with his tongue and drove off. For ten minutes we dashed along, rolled along. The loose-limbed carriage swayed dangerously from left to right. Every two or three minutes we nearly ran into something. Every other two or three minutes something nearly ran into us. The Italian drives with a magnificent indifference to everything. He just makes his horses go and leaves the rest to fate. But his trust in fate is deep, for he makes his horses tear along crowded streets as if there was nothing to be avoided.

As we drove we passed gay streams of carriages taking people to the theatre, to the opera. We saw two carriages lose a wheel each as they bumped into other carriages. A little swearing, a general scattering of diabolic frowns, and then – but we have passed on.

Suddenly our driver stopped.

'Go on!' cried Jean.

'Go on!' cried I.

He turned and gabbled something at us. We understood that he wanted to know where he was to go. Where then had we been going all this time?

'*Boat!*' cried Jean. 'Steamer, *Orient – Orientale.*'

'*Le vaisseau*,' I piped in.

He shook his head.

'The wharf,' said Jean.

'The water,' said I.

'*Parlez vous francais*?' said Jean.

He understood none of it. We began to be alarmed. Then we remembered our little steamer tickets. Jean gave him hers to read.

'I suppose he knows his own language,' said we.

He took the ticket, looked at it, and started off. For another ten minutes we tore along through the gaily lighted streets – but *where?*

He stopped again.

'*Go on!*' we cried piteously now. But he shook his head, got down and disappeared into a shop, the paper ticket in his hand.

After some moments, in which Jean and I sat and boiled, he came out, followed by half-a-dozen men, all talking away together. They took a deep interest in us, but we understood nothing of what they were saying. All we wanted was our boat, and now we began to be frightened. There were fifteen minutes left to us, and it took ten to row from the wharf to our steamer.

'You must go on,' said Jean. She pointed sternly in front of her with a little terracotta baby, whose brown feet stuck out through the tissue paper as if they, too, were possessed with our desire to proceed. We said all the words over again, and he clicked his tongue again, and again started off, only to tear up and down two or three streets and stop again.

This time he ran into a restaurant and brought out a French waiter. Then we understood that all this time he had been trying to read the ticket or get someone else to read it, so that we had just as likely been going to Pompeii as to our vessel.

Feverish explanations and entreaties. We brought forth all our French, all our power of persuasion. '*Le vapeur,*' said the waiter. He read the ticket, with half-a-dozen quickly assembled Neapolitans looking over his shoulder. Then he talked to our driver for a minute and light seemed to gleam on that parched creature's senses. Jean gave the waiter a shilling, the driver clicked and we started off again.

Quicker than ever this time. 'We'll do it, we'll just do it.' And we might have *just* done it, only that next minute a carriage, driving gaily towards us, had dashed into our right side, and we saw one of our wheels trundling off along the street.

A volley of foreign language thickened the air. Our carriage hopped along for sixty seconds on three legs and then stopped. With this last stoppage we lost our heads, lost our tempers, lost our manners. We jumped out. We recognised the street – the wharf was three minutes away. We flew towards it. It seemed to us as if everyone in Naples was after us. Our driver certainly was; we had not paid him, we were too angry to be just. All we thought of was the boat, the boat. We flew through the customs house, through the far passage, across the wharf. There was no steam tender, everything had gone.

'*Omrac!*' cried Jean.

'*Omrac!*' cried I.

Three boatmen seized us by the arm, dragged us into a little rowing boat. We were out on the dark bay before we knew what had happened. They were all talking together, telling us they would catch it for us. They looked capable of cutting us up into little pieces and throwing us overboard, but they were all we had, so we put our faith in them. We promised them a sovereign if they would catch it. We raised our voices and sent long cooees across the dim, shadowy waters. It seemed as if our boat, with her gay, yellow lights throbbing into the stream, was *moving*. Our cooees grew frantic. The

Neapolitans joined in with great, rich voices, crying like big children, '*Omerac! Omerac!* Come back, *Om-er-ac.*' And suddenly *Om-er-ac* slipped, in the sneakiest way, round the corner and was gone.

'Can, not, find,' said one of our guides mournfully. He was the one who knew a little English. The others all agreed in their own language.

And there we were, stranded. Two lone Australian women in a strange land. To Englishwomen it would have been nothing, perhaps, but to us, never out of Australia before, it was an appalling disaster.

'Is there a train tonight?' asked Jean. '*Train* – locomotive.'

It is always the word you never use that foreigners understand. They all brightened up at locomotive, and gave us to understand there was one. They seemed so sorry that I began to laugh. This looked unseemly, so I put my head down in my hands and pretended to cry.

'Don't cry,' said Jean, entering into the feeble joke. I couldn't stop crying, but out of one corner watched the two boatmen who didn't know English gesture to the one who did. They were evidently asking him to give me a little comfort in English.

'Lady,' said he, in a voice of intense sweetness, '*la Bella Napoli!*'

He pointed to the starry sky, and Vesuvius and the Siren City. The others all cheered up suddenly, and pointed also to the sky, and Vesuvius and the city.

'*La Bella Napoli!*' they all murmured, rolling their great black eyes round the scene.

It was so pretty and novel to my Australian mind.

Imagine any English-speaking boatman cheering a 'fare' by calling before him the beauty of nature.

Greatly consoled, I ceased crying. But this was no time to play the fool. It was a terrible thing that had happened. Yet I never had such an utterly ecstatic feeling as coming back from that deserting vessel. Is there such a thing as a well-regulated mind that takes pleasure only in things marked pleasure? Or are we all liable to sudden confusions when terrors turn to delights, and frightfully annoying and unexpected things set our brains leaping violently in a kind of ecstasy?

There we were, down near the foot of Italy, with no luggage, no Italian, not a soul to help us, and perhaps no money. We had, neither of us, ever been out of Australia before. We wouldn't even know London when we saw it, if we ever saw it. It was night. And we were out alone on the Bay of Naples with three cutthroat foreigners, who had seen us miss our steamer and knew we were unprotected and in a plight.

And there was my wretched little heart singing and chirruping away like a bird. My spirits had gone up and up and soared high above me. I was glad we had missed the boat, even while I was decorously echoing Jean's sentiments that this was an *awful* thing to happen to us!

Well, our rowers brought us back safely to the wharf, but their villainous expressions were justified when we came to pay them. They said we had promised them a sovereign *each*. We treated this with quaking scorn, and Jean held out one sovereign, pointing to the three men in succession. Of course a crowd gathered round us. Dark faces were poked over our shoulders and everyone had a say in the matter. They all gesticulated and smiled sweetly on us, but all took sides against us, as if they had heard all that had passed between us and the boatmen.

'Not another penny,' said Jean. 'I said if you *caught* the boat, and you didn't catch it.'

We hurried away, followed by the crowd, who came right out into the street with us. We jumped into a carriage and managed two words, '*Locomotive stazione*', not at all sure that the crowd would let us go. It did, however, but the last we saw of the poetic-souled boatmen who had bid me look to the sky and stars for comfort, was a tossing of contemptuous arms after us, a lot of angry words, and three horrible expressions of hatred and scorn. I think, on the whole, I prefer working men who can't roll up reverent eyes to the beauty above them. They are more likely to have a square system in their breasts.

It was about ten o'clock when we reached the railway station. In the meantime we discovered between us ten sovereigns. We had no idea of the cost of the journey. For all we knew it might have been twenty pounds each. But Jean's spirits were catching fire from mine. Seeing me so happy and so exhilarated she began to think she might as well get all the fun out of the situation there was to be got, so she, too, began to bubble up in the mercurial manner of our countrywomen, and we arrived at the station as gay as larks.

The first thing to do was to get a timetable and find out if there was a train to Marseilles that night, and what time it started, and what time it got there. The station had an unkempt and gloomy look. We went to the bookstall, found a timetable, and bought it. It was all in Italian, very small print, and quite unintelligible to us. The trains seemed to start at twenty-five minutes past twenty-four, or fifteen minutes past fourteen. We went to a porter, but he knew neither French nor English. He called another porter who knew no more and had less intelligence.

It was then that I came to the conclusion that it is a mistake to begin to learn a language. I had begun to learn Italian and gone on several months. In my head I could see little paths running down masculine and feminine articles, and singulars and plurals.

The nouns I could think of were *coltello*, *acqua*, *padre*. I also remembered *si*.

If only I could get something to fit *si* on to. But no. I had no opportunity of getting *coltello* into anything, and as for *padre*, there was nobody about who seemed likely to play that part to us.

At last, after a lot of gesturing and bold glances from the most un-porterish eyes I ever saw, one man went away to find an interpreter. Guards – of all men – generally wear a neat, impersonal look in their eyes. After some time he came back with a boy in a blue suit and little peaked cap.

'A square chin,' murmured Jean.

We both felt relieved. He was as honest, earnest-looking a boy as you could meet in your own country. His eyes were a light hazel brown, clear and straightforward. We felt we could trust him. He knew a very little English, a very little French, and I suppose a lot of Italian. Yes, there was very little Italian he did not know.

We told him everything. How we had lost our boat and wanted to catch it at Marseilles. How ignorant we were of the language. How we couldn't understand the timetable. How we wanted to know the fares.

All, all he would tell us. The art of understanding as little as you please was thoroughly mastered by our new friend. He first explained how much our tickets would cost for the through journey from Naples to Marseilles, by way of Rome, Genoa, Ventimiglia. They would be four pounds each. That was easy enough to grasp. We grasped it.

He then left that subject and turned to the question of the train. He drilled it into our foggy minds that the train started at half past eleven, and got to Rome early in the morning. There we changed trains and went on to Genoa. There we changed trains again and went on to Ventimiglia. There we changed trains yet again and went on to Marseilles.

'And shall we catch our ship – *le vapeur*?' we asked; great stress on *le vapeur* now we had got hold of it.

Oh, yes, we would catch *le vapeur*. We asked him if people always caught it. He replied that people always did. After that there was nothing else to hear.

Then he returned to the question of the cost of tickets. He had just told us these would be four pounds each. Now he took hold of our train book and began to scribble figures on the cover. He gave us to understand there would be something more. He made a lot of little figures and then expounded them. As far as we could gather four pounds was the price, and then there was a strange something else, a nameless something else, which would amount to about another pound.

We wanted to know why this was so. But his English and his French both failed him there. The more he talked the less we understood. The ticket office was shut still.

Then he began to get back a little English. He told us that we had better first get our money changed into Italian money. If we came with him. So we went with him.

He walked along the dreary railway station with its dim lights. He wore a dark blue suit and a porter's cap. Besides, he had dog's eyes and a square chin. We followed without a qualm. We thought he was taking us to another part of the station. We went along merrily, both in the highest spirits now. We *seemed* to be out in the city, crossing a street, but in our utter ignorance we thought it must be an opening in the station. At last he went through a doorway, looking to see we came after him. Now we found ourselves in a crowded room, full of men all playing round little tables. Our guard went through them to a counter at the far end. He had a brief conversation in his own language with an old Italian whose nose and eyes seemed to *scream* at us. We fancied that he did not want to change our money, but our friend told us the change would be effected, and would we please give our English money. Jean and I emptied our purses on the counter. Our ten sovereigns were clutched by Shylock[7] and put away in a drawer. Then paper money began to be counted out to us.

Here, and not till here, a feeling of insecurity came over us. Why were we changing *all* our money? Why could not the ticket office change it? Where on earth were we? And who were these men?

I looked over my shoulder, and, behold! All the men in the place had left their gambling tables and had come up close behind us. Some of them were awful ruffians, some were poor fools. But all wore one common expression directed at us – amusement. Why were we so entertaining?

'There's something wrong,' said I. 'We won't change. They're cheating us.'

Really, I shiver now as I think how I boldly entered into that controversy. I pushed the paper away and said we wanted our money back. Our friend turned reproachful eyes on me. Shylock tried to combine winning-ness

---

[7] The moneylender in William Shakespeare's *The Merchant of Venice*.

with malice. Our friend said we couldn't travel without changing. Why not? Well, it wasn't safe with gold. Then why could not the ticket office change? Again, English and French failed him. All he could tell us was that we must change.

'Give us our money back, please,' said I.

Without turning, I could feel the smiles passing round those horrid, inquisitive faces so close behind us.

'We want our money *back*,' said Jean, a little louder. Shylock then began an animated row with Square Chin. They seemed to be saying very nasty things to each other in Italian – about us, we were quite sure. But the Australian spirit, set free in a new sphere, is merged with such confidence, such boldness, such ignorance, that it never occurred to us to be frightened. It would have been a great surprise to us if they had robbed us and cut our throats. To some women it would have been a greater surprise that they did not.

But they did not. We were so positive we would get our money back that we got it. Yes, every gold coin came clinking back to us out of that drawer. I believe there was one moment when our fates were in danger. It is nice to believe so, anyway. But in that minute Jean said to me, in English, 'The *idea* of that *fellow* bringing us to a place like this! How *dare* he have such an *impertinence*! Pretending he was taking us to the proper railway office! I *never* heard of such a thing! I wish *Alfred* was here!' with such staccato emphasis that they probably thought we had some scheme up our sleeves. Shylock threw the money at us as if he were throwing stones in our faces. We laid a shilling on the counter and went calmly out, our heads well in the air. At the door we heard loud bursts of language and laughter. There was evidently a great joke as well as great wrath left behind.

'Take us *straight* to the ticket office,' said Jean to Square Chin.

I had been watching him curiously. It was quite interesting to see the change that had been coming over his face; gradually the dog in his eyes had been disappearing. A fox had begun to show itself. The cool, calm, sincere look had turned into one of warm cunning. Even the shape of the eye had altered. It had grown smaller – and was destined to grow smaller yet.

At the ticket office began the most audacious bit of trickery conceivable. The little window was open now. I went to it myself.

'Do you take English gold?' I asked in French – from Sydney.

Square Chin flashed a long sentence in over my shoulder. The man at the window sent him back another.

'Yes, he will take your gold,' said Square Chin. 'It will be eight pounds, and then there will be,' and he held up the figures on the timetable again. He now represented to us we would have to pay one pound each in addition to our railway fare. We appealed to the ticket office official. But what was the use of appealing to him? Backwards and forwards flashed telegraphic messages over our heads from the man at the window and our interpreter.

'It will leave us nothing,' said Jean, blandly.

'I know they are cheating us,' said I. Other creatures joined in. It was like an Irish fair when the third party tries to do the business; ever so many third parties gathered round. And just then, oh, the joy of it! A big man came along and made his way to our window. We had moved out of the little railed passage to discuss our situation. We heard him order his ticket. He spoke Italian, but there was a something about him that we *caught* at.

'Do you know English?' asked Jean.

Oh, blessed sound!

'Yes, can I do anything for you?' answered he.

How we poured out our story! How angry he looked, and sometimes how amused!

'They tell us eight pounds. Why do they want to make us pay forty shillings more?'

Dear me! How one big man can disturb things. To our comfort, be it said. He turned and shed Italian abroad left and right. He was evidently in a great rage. They, of course, explained themselves their way, but our big man would have none of their explanation. He told us that, of course, they were trying to cheat us, all the lot of them. He bought our tickets himself – four pounds each and no mysterious something else.

'Do you know where your train goes from? No? Well, I'm going up to Rome myself. Time is nearly up. I will guide you, if you'll allow me.'

Oh, nice, big, broad-shouldered Englishman, how meekly we followed you! Square Face by this time had completely changed. If ever there was a discomfited rogue it was he. Craft was written all over his face. I suppose he puts that sincere dog-look on whenever he meets Australian women wandering about alone.

Oh, nice, big Englishman, how we blessed you! He hadn't a dog-look – just a jolly, kind-man look. We decided it was much better. And he put us into our train. How nice it was to know we were really in the train we wanted to be in, to have no qualms. We were in a little compartment with two other women, a French lady and her daughter.

'I travel in the smoker,' said our friend. 'If you'll allow me, I'll come and look for you in the morning when we get to Rome.'

'Thank you so much! Thank you *so* much.'

'We knew you were English as soon as we heard you speak Italian,' said I, leaning out of the window.

He laughed a big, breezy laugh.

'Oh, my Italian's jolly fine,' said he.

Then off he went, and we saw him no more that night.

It was nearly midnight as we started. The little French ladies packed themselves up neatly on their side, and Jean and I screwed ourselves along our seat. I rested my head on Jean's feet. Horrid little feet I called them that night.

Off went the train, and soon we all slept. Such a funny, hot-headed sleep, and every now and then a semi-consciousness, in which I whispered to myself, 'You're in Italy, you're going up to Rome,' and myself whispered back to me, 'Nonsense, how can you tell such stories?'

But we were.

Early morning, before dawn broke, a green world gleamed outside our window. My heart began to beat madly. There was surprise mixed with the wild beatings.

I had anticipated brown and grey ruins, and ruins, and ruins, and ruins. Here were green fields, and the fire of a million scarlet poppies blazing from fields and roadsides. Except for the poppies and the great grey walls, I could have believed myself going from Launceston to Hobart, nearing Hobart. That's the first great lesson of travelling. The world is just the world. A city is just a city. Land is just land. Grass is just grass. Trees are just trees. The dream place doesn't exist, nor the dream trees, nor the dream atmosphere. Perhaps it is on account of all my dream cities that my first attitude to each new land is antagonism. They are only cities after all, and it hurts to find that out, and to find that it *is* a truth, and there's no getting away from it except by death.

I didn't expect to find marble emperors stalking about marble streets in purple state. But I didn't expect a railway station and buns and coffee at *Rome!* Trains at *Rome!*

I am glad I am writing to you – yous, as Sir 'Enry 'Anson would say – because yous won't know any better than I knew, and yous won't be astonished that I was astonished to find that people go to Rome by train.

Other people might say, 'But surely if you had *thought!*' Yes, but that's just it. We didn't think. When by some unlikely chance our thoughts turned Rome-wards, we left the way of arriving there hidden in a vague mist. We were not even conscious of the mist. In fact, we scarcely believed that Rome *is*. And it is. Oh, yes. I went up to it and away from it in the second-class carriage of a railway train one night, one lovely night in May.

During the night we made the acquaintance of the French lady and her daughter. In one's early days one is apt to tell everybody one comes from Australia. I suppose we had already let the secret escape. Now with the dawn began a conversation with the recumbent forms opposite. The girl looked fresh as a daisy. She had a fair, round face. A sleepless night in a railway train had made her positively fairer and rounder and fresher than ever. She bloomed out of the hood of her black-and-white checked cloak, and her eyes were as clear and bright, and her skin as pure, as if she had come back from a bath after a long night's sleep.

As I looked at her I thought of those charming lines of my beloved Victor Daley's:

> If I were young as you, Sixteen,
> And you were old as I—
> I would not be as I have been
> You would not be so shy.[8]

And the terrible antiquity attached to twenty-one made me envious, almost jealous. Twenty-one! Twenty-one! An age when you cannot travel all night half-sleeplessly without turning yellow in the morning. And partly it was her simple, young French expression, so different from the expression of us at sixteen – highly strung, highly nervous, feeling keenly, and wearing all the signs of feelings on our tense young faces. So even if I *had* been sixteen I could not have looked as she did, unruffled, smooth, unworn.

The conversation turned on Australia. This was the first time we heard a quaint criticism on our country.

Said the mother, 'You haf a griite deal of dosst there, is it not?'

Said the girl, with a sympathetic expression, worn on our behalf, 'Terrible the duss there, are they not?'

It took us some time to realise that the reputation our country had gained abroad was so largely built on dust. We had not looked upon Australia as a particularly dusty place before, but it was not the only time we heard that comment upon our island continent. The legend springs probably from the legends of our drynesses and droughts,

---

[8] From Victor Daley's 'Sixty to Sixteen', in *At Dusk and Dawn* (1898; reprinted 1902). Daley was a poet and journalist, well known for his contributions to the *Bulletin*.

kept in good repair by our poets. The one, for instance, who sang so plaintively,

> I hope that I shall never be
> As dry as Lake Eliza.[9]

I pressed my face to the windowpane, and saw the Campagna coming nearer and nearer in the pale light of early morn.

I made a few desperate efforts to adjust two sets of thoughts, one belonging to the imagined Rome, existing all these years only in the mind, and one leaping from this actual Rome. There was not so much a want of harmony between the two as a natural estrangement between two who had never met and never anticipated meeting. I tried to understand that it was to Rome we were coming, but in vain. That great desolate field on the right of the railway line, and away in the distance the silhouetted city, red with dawn, was that indeed the Campagna? Was that indeed Rome?

I wonder are we more than a little hysterical as travellers, we Australians, packed away there at the other end of the world, shut off from all that is great in art and music, but born with a passionate craving to see, and hear, and come close to these great things and their homes.

Most of us are born of English parents. Fused in our compositions are Old World sights, and sounds, and dreams, and memories, and the auras of great people and places.

You, Mamma, nearly 'saw Shelley plain'. That is to say, you heard your father talk of walking with Shelley one

---

[9] From Henry Lawson's 'Lake Eliza', first published in the *Bulletin*, 16 December 1893.

day in a wood at Avenza. You glowed at the thought, and transmitted the glow to me before I was born. But there was reality to you in the memory. You had seen your father, who had walked with Shelley, and you had seen the country in which Shelley was born, whereas your relating of that episode aroused in me, born twelve thousand miles away, nothing but a purely spiritual delight, flashing from an image of a sudden contact with the spirit of Shelley, whose material existence refused to enter into my conceptions. I glowed with twice as bright a fire as yours. Those twelve thousand miles had carried away all the reality. Nothing remained for me but a glorious pang, and if I analysed that pang I should find, surely, that its keenest sweetness came as it pierced me with an image of the impossible become possible, but still remaining impossible – of Shelley, who was never real, being seen in the real by my grandfather, but still remaining to me an intangible force, of whose actuality I could never be assured.

Twelve thousand miles removes Australians into a realm of such ardent hero-worship as no peoples living nearer the world's centre could ever understand. After a lifetime of vivid imagination and earnest adoration, we are conscious of great shocks when we travel and come right up to our vague, glorified dreams. Everything is too much for us to realise. It is like meeting continually arrays of glorious, resurrected ghosts.

~

Jean and I planned a lovely programme for Rome. We thought we should have only a few hours there. Tired as we were, we meant to rush to St Peter's, see as many pictures and statues as possible, dash into the Catacombs, drive on the Appian Way. We also included hot baths and breakfast in our plans.

It was just seven as we steamed into Rome railway station. Tired, dirty, hungry, hot-headed, but intensely happy, we alighted and ran into our nice big Englishman coming to find us.

'You have just ten minutes to drink a cup of coffee in, and eat a bun, before your train starts,' was what he said.

Away with all our dreams of hot baths and St Peter's and the Catacombs! He hurried us across the railway lines, which we walked across primitively, as they do at Burraburroo, without overhead bridge or underground tunnel, and put us into another train. Then he brought a waiter and we ordered coffee and rolls, and in a twinkling there was a big tray at the train door.

O tempora! O mores! O Rome, and buns, and coffee! My memory of Rome will ever bring before me the best coffee and the most curiously enticing bun I ever met, a little sweet, light, crisp, melting round thing, as unlike a bun as this Rome was unlike my other private-property-Rome.

Buns, coffee, Rome! Rome, buns, coffee! Coffee, Rome, buns! However you place them they won't look right.

So I'll hasten away from them, away from Rome, away from our nice big Englishman. He gave Jean his card. His name is Gerald Huntley. Jean gave him her hotel address in London. We hope to meet him again, the dear, big thing who saved us from the brigands.

We bought a lunch-basket before the train started. No food ever gave me such delight. There were so many mysterious little packages in white paper to explore.

Sticking out of one end was a bottle of Italian wine, and out of the rear a bottle of Aqua di Roma, to be taken *after* the meal, I suppose, but we threw it out of the window. Oranges and purple grapes gave tone to the basket. A long crisp loaf gave reality. In the little packets we found cold chicken, cold sausage, cold 'rosbif', butter, cheese, pepper and salt, and some little iced cakes that nearly melted as you looked at them, and serviettes of paper, folded capriciously and standing carefully high up out of the hamper. Over all waved a little green flag, a purely decorative addition. There was also a highly ornamental little knife with a handle of bright green wood and a folding blade, not too beautiful and proud to cut up our chicken and beef and cheese.

Meanwhile, outside the window there was a note from home for us.

Rows of gum trees stood on the banks to each side of the railway lines, sad, seared, alien trees, suffering badly from homesickness and frost, but very dear to us. They stirred our heartstrings, poor lonely ones, so far away from home and the Great Silence. We saw many of them outside Rome, and more about Civitavecchia, gazing away sadly across the Mediterranean. Oh, such long, lean trees they were! Such appealing scarecrows of trees! What else could they be, brought from their own homes and asked to protect the oily Italians against fevers – for that is what they are there for. My heart ached so that I had to make myself hard, and eat 'rosbif' and drink *fiaschetto vino* to help me to forget them.

The other passengers in the carriage were three – an old Italian gentleman and his old brown wife, in a brown dress, and thick woolly brown gloves, and a young Frenchman.

The latter jumped in just as the train was starting. He was in a startling state of newness and smartness, the most dapper little man that ever hurried to catch a train and fell over my feet in the catching of it. He was so funny, so droll, so small, so compact, finished, and fierce, with his black moustache waxed like two black lucifers on either side of his little, stiff, white nose, with his small feet encased in frightfully shiny little boots of patent leather, with his thin legs in the tightest of striped grey trousers, belonging to an equally well-fitting, short, grey coat, so unlike anything I had ever seen before, that I could not keep my eyes off him. He was the first Frenchman I had ever seen out of Australia, and he seemed to me to be in some ways like Jean and me – that is to say, he was conspicuously a countryman of his own country.

Presently, through staring so hard, I capsized the basket, which knocked over my bag; all my money rolled out. Some of it went behind the seat, some fell on the floor. Jean and I tried to gather it together, but we found we must raise the seat before we could reach the coins between the seat and the back of the carriage. We had to ask the Italian gentleman to get up. He did so as if we were conferring the largest fortune on him he had ever received, and proceeded to help us lift the long velvet cushion.

Suddenly, up jumped the little Frenchman and hurriedly joined in the search. He went down on his knees, and dived into the shady corners that lurk beneath the seats in railway carriages, and presently he came up with several coins in his grasp, and with two very dusty little hands.

To us, the dust on them was only dust. To him it seemed a tragedy, without the climax of the last act – without any last act, in fact.

He seated himself, when all the money was restored to me, and sadly held out his hands before him and looked at them. For full five minutes he stared at them. His expression was indescribable. It revealed horror, but the other emotions were unknown to us – or at any rate we could not recognise them in that guise. There he sat, gazing at those little dusty hands, as if hell had been suddenly let loose between his fingers. It was evidently a terrible crisis to him. He seemed as if he could not rise above it. The longer he looked, the more complicated grew his expression. He seemed as if he were going to die of disgust.

By and by he jumped up and stared out of the window. I think he was trying to forget his hands. But every now and then I saw his eyes go down towards them; then out they would go, the two offended members. The fingers were held stiffly out, and his gaze remained on them for many minutes at a time. I was likely to die with suppressed laughter.

Sometimes for a quarter of an hour he forgot. He dozed, or looked at the scenery. Then recollection would overtake him, and out would go his hands, and over his tiny, waxed, washed, tidied countenance would steal that look of suppressed wrath and horror.

This went on for hours. We passed Pontegal, Fiumicino, Ponte Galeria, Maccarese, Palidoro, Palo, Santa Severa, Santa Marinella, and still he looked at his hands.

I tried to get some information from him. I wanted to know whether our train left us any time at Genoa before the other train started to take us to Marseilles. I tried in English. Failure. Tried again in French. Scarcely a success. Then he took a bit of paper and a pencil from his pocket and offered them to me. And I wrote down, '*Allons-nous en de Genoa a la même heure dans lequel nous arriverons a Genoa.'*

And he didn't understand still, and never did, not even to this day – nor do I at this day, though I thought I did at that time.

And he never had anything to eat all that long, long day! I have read in the *Family Herald* of men feeding on the looks of a lovely woman in dead white with golden hair or violets, but he was my first instance of anyone feeding all day on a pair of dirty hands – his own, to wit. We all ate and drank at intervals. He never did. Sometimes he jumped out at one of the stations and walked quickly up and down with a furious scowl, robbed of intimidation by his dapper neatness that never failed him except in one particular. Every time he returned his little black hat was more and more on one side.

What was he, this little man? Merely, it may be, a vivid picture of strange life offered us by the gods who were illustrating our travels. That explanation might not satisfy him, but it is all I have to offer on my own behalf. His own translation of himself is not likely to reach me. I shall go curious to my life's end, whenever I happen to think of him, see him staring at his dirty hands with angry eyes, watch his white cheeks grow slowly redder and redder, note his eyes gaining a fierce sparkle, see him take his energetic dives out on to the platform, dash up and down in haste with his hat on one side for several minutes, but never take a cup of coffee or a glass of wine, and then return with a redder cheek, a crookeder hat, and a wilder eye, to resume at intervals that inspection of his hands. All these I shall see, but shall never see behind them. He was a mystery, he is a mystery, and there is nothing more to say of him than that he completed the picture.

What a strange day for us! Out of the windows went flying by Italy – Italy, mountains, fields, castles, villages, cities, and all day long on our left lay the Mediterranean, not a shimmering field of gay wide blue, but a leaden sea tossing greyly against the land. It was so close sometimes that we could throw a stone into it from our train.

Rain fell. Sometimes we slept and sometimes watched, and the strange day went on.

Away to the right lay the mountains, never many miles away. It was Italy truly, but it was all so much less beautiful than I had expected. What was missing? Perhaps the light that never was on sea or land. *Italy!* The word was stored with too strong a magic. In the land itself the magic faded or hid until it was found. It did not give itself for the glance as the name gave for the utterance.

And then there was something else – something that came between me and Italy, and comes still. Even as I write it rises up, and I can't help myself. I turn myself away, away from the land I have loved, and wandered in, in dreams, for years. This something never entered into my dream-travels. No one ever made me realise it. The poets left it out of their poetry.

It was, prosaically put, the smell of Italy that turned me traitor.

What an odour! Sweet, oh, horribly sweet! How shall I describe it? Orange blossoms and gardenias, and honeysuckles and magnolias, mixed with an indescribable smell of rottenness. It followed us everywhere, that deadly mingling of sweet and foul, of flowers and dustbins and rotting vegetables. It stole across me every time I put my head out of the window; it was in the carriage, it floated round the railway stations. At last it made me mad.

'Oh, you horrible country!' I said in my heart, and began a piteous prayer for England, where surely there was to be found a good clean odour that one could live in.

It was penetrating, insistent. It breathed with a morbid sickliness of death and tuberoses. All the way from Naples, through the Italian Riviera, it chased us. It was wafted in from those wonderful old gardens of palaces along the Mediterranean where flowers and trees grow in such heavy luxuriance that their beauty takes on a spirit of insolence, perhaps from the dead, proud people who have wandered there, as well as from the wealth of flowers and trees. Even the great wide plains and the pine woods we rushed through, and the blackish-grey groves of olive continually passing us, gave out this ugly perfume. Possibly some of the sickliness was due to garlic, but fresh flowers and rotting vegetables recurred to the mind with every breath, until at last my consciousness resolved itself into such unbearable longing to get out into a new *clean* country with wholesome unscented air.

In the meantime we were passing through Italy as quickly as possible. Our train rushed on. Green slopes and plains, purple valleys and blue mountains to our right: the grey sea to our left. And the names that flashed by us, every one carrying its thrill to the heart's core – Civitavecchia, Orbetello, Volterra, Cecina, Santa Luce, Livorno, Pisa.

Our compartment had long formed itself into a family party. What an intimacy is established between half-a-dozen people travelling all day in a railway carriage when stiffness does not happen to be an intruder. How keen the interest in each other. How closely scanned are the faces around, until something of their lives is discovered by the searching eyes that read them. Soon everyone knew we were from Australia, had missed our boat, and were tearing on to catch it at Marseilles, if luck was in our favour. An Englishwoman in a tam-o'-shanter with a thin nose, and her English husband with the moustache of a lord and blue eyes, got in at Orbetello, and showed how little they thought of themselves by taking notice of us.

The Englishwoman made rather a droll remark.

'Whenever I used to see an animal in the zoo with "Australia" on its cage I always thought, "What a long way you have come from!"'

That was meant to be pretty. (What do 'yous' think?)

Another couple got in at Pisa. The train stopped there for a quarter of an hour. Jean and I were out on the station having a cup of coffee at the buffet, and buying those little white models of the Leaning Tower. When we went back to the carriage our seats were taken. A man and a woman were occupying them.

'Pardon me, these are our seats,' said Jean, politely.

They looked at us in silence; they did not move.

'We have been sitting there all day,' said Jean.

They took no notice beyond gazing at her.

A loud bell rang; we had to get in. There was nowhere for us to sit together. Jean took a backward seat, and I sat down between the intruders and the English husband and wife. We were annoyed. Someone might have saved our seats for us.

The English wife said we should have put some luggage on them before we got out. She did not mean to be sarcastic. Most people *do* have luggage when travelling about the Continent. It was not her fault that we had nothing but the purses in our hands.

There was nothing but to endure. We could no longer change places at the window and take it in turn to stare out at the strange world beyond, with its constant succession of vivid little pictures, so fascinating, so dramatic. Sometimes we cried aloud at the sight of dark-haired women washing clothes in the flat brown river between low flat banks; at a long line of thin black poplars bowed by the wind right across a landscape; at a grey chateau on a hillside, with romance even on the outside; at the queer 'railway stations', where the train simply stopped in front of a big two-storey house, almost on the line, and heads of women, men and children appeared at the upper windows or the doors.

'Isn't it horrid of them?' said Jean to me.

'Nasty mean things,' said I, in the security of English.

I sat next the male usurper. Between us was the arm dividing his seat from mine. I rested my elbow on it and dozed. In my sleep something pushed me gently, gently. My elbow slipped off the cushioned arm. I woke sharply. The man had his arm there. It was he who had pushed mine off.

I looked round. Everyone had gone to sleep. We had all exhausted ourselves in the long, straining glimpses of the pale Tower of Pisa away to the right, leaning dizzily, and wholly visible to the eyes of tram travellers. For several minutes we were able to gaze and take it in.

'Might shall *not* be right,' I said to myself. I put my arm back on its legitimate rest. It was again pushed off with gentleness, but positively. This happened three times. Everyone else slept. The little man had his little hat over his little nose, his little mouth was half open under his little black moustache, his shining little feet were crossed and his dirty little hands were still at last. The Englishwoman was leaning against her husband's arm; he was inclining towards his window. Jean was sheltering beneath her hat, although her pose was as upright as ever. The old brown Italian lady and gentleman had placed their feet on a brown portmanteau, covered their faces with handkerchiefs and fled this waking life.

Outside the window went flying by lovely glimpses. The sun was out. The sea was shining. And oh, the gleam of the wet olives and deep promises of the pine woods by the sea!

I tried to put myself in touch with the sweet things outside and forget my unpleasant companion. In vain. I was too tired. Four weeks and thousands of strange miles at sea; a long day, beginning before daybreak, in a strange city; a long night travelling in a strange country; another long day crowded with a continual succession of startling and vivid impressions, all these had combined to wear my nervous energy to too fine a point. I was nearly exhausted. To lay my head down for five minutes would have been indescribable happiness. Empty as it was it seemed too heavy to keep up. Again I leaned my elbow on the armrest and dropped my head sideways in my hand. A feeling of great calm came over me at once. I was just asleep when off slipped my elbow again. There was that great fellow leaning his elbow there, sleeping, or pretending to be asleep, and pushing me off at the same time.

Tired, cross, aggravated, I sat bolt upright and gave way to a feeling of hatred.

Then I took a paper serviette from our basket, opened it wide and quietly slipped it down between his arm and mine.

I meant it to be a gentle hint and a deadly insult combined. It was not a very nice thing to do, I know. But I didn't feel nice. I was not myself or anyone related to me at that moment.

Jean opened her eyes at that moment, saw my action, and was first petrified, then amused.

'This horrible person pushes my arm off whenever I go to sleep,' I said in a low voice.

I turned my head and saw that he was looking down at the piece of paper between us. But after that I was left in peace. My arm remained there and I slept on my hand, the most divine sleep I can remember.

The hours went on. It was mid-afternoon. We were flying through lovely places. It was raining again, but there were pale bursts of sun. We passed Carrara and saw the pink marble lying out in the wet. We saw the colour of rose it lent to the near hillsides.

There began an endless succession of tunnels. The Englishman came out as a hero. He sat at the window and slashed it up and down until I grew positively dizzy with counting. I wondered his arm did not crack. Up and down, up and down. No sooner had he opened it than we were in another tunnel, and up it came again. Why did he not leave it down? Why did he not leave it up? Why did he work us all up to a state of nervous frenzy, unable to resist watching his operations? His face wore an expression of mild determination mixed with stupidity. I thought: is he indifferent to our scorn? Or is he impenetrable?

Yes, he was impenetrable. There was only room for one idea at a time in his John Bull head. We had been warned in Australia to look out for this kind of thing, but did not expect to encounter it so quickly. The one idea in his head at present was to open and shut that window.

How he grappled with the tunnels. He had been here before. But sometimes he miscalculated, and the tunnel would roar upon him while the window was still down, and we would hear him slashing through the dark, with the leather strap in his hand. And sometimes the tunnels followed each other in almost breathless succession, one after the other, one after the other, and the window would then be in such a condition of darting up only to be flung down, that a white despair settled in a mist of tears over its panes, and it gave up all hope of ever again finding out whether it was open or shut that day.

La Spezia, Riomaggiore, Monterosso, Levanto, Bonassola, Chiavari, Rapallo, Santa Margherita, all with their faces to the Mediterranean. And sun and rain, and a sparkling world of sea on one side and green land on the other. Then sun, and a clear sky of azure.

A sky less blue than ours, even though rain-deepened. Not the great ineffable fire of turquoise that shines over Sydney half the year round, but a paler, softer blue.

Many a place calls to me as we pass, 'Come back, come back.' I fly on with a pang. I would like to linger with some of these haunting spots. But we pass on.

These are the quickest friendships I ever made. Only a minute's glimpse, yet I remember their faces and know I want them again. They all have definite places in my heart and brain, though I cannot call them all by name.

We were near Genoa. Everyone was wide awake. Questions were flying round. Jean and I tried to get information about our trains. We were beginning to wonder now what would happen if we lost our boat. The other passengers joined in the discussion. Some thought it was possible. Others thought not. No one knew anything about it.

Here the man who had taken my seat, and pushed my arm off the rest, and who had spoken French up till now, astounded Jean and me by addressing us in the most English English, and with the greatest suavity.

'I have a timetable here,' he said, 'and I find that you will be in Genoa about six, and leave at nine to catch the train to Marseilles. *Plenty* of time.'

Three hours! How we rejoiced in the thought of them. A rest at last. Hot baths, dinner, and a long drive round Genoa. Then we could bravely face the long night's train journey still before us. In our present state of fatigue and faintness it was appalling. We thanked him, and he smiled, a queer smile. I remembered his smile afterwards.

Genoa at last, a great city of gardens and palaces. A sad city, looking as if she had been left behind at the sea's edge, with all her splendours faded. A city of architecture, but lonely.

Goodbye to the old lady and gentleman who came all the way from Rome with us; goodbye to the little man, who will ever fill us with curiosity; goodbye to the lady in her tam-o'-shanter, whom we reminded of the zoo; goodbye to her husband, with the pale determined eyes; goodbye to the foreign man and his wife who had stolen our seats; goodbye, *goodbye*.

Will you believe it? We parted from them with regret! They all hoped that we would catch our boat. 'Adieu!' they cried.

They went on to Turin. We ran up the steps from the station as gay as larks, as light as air. No wonder, considering how little we had eaten since yesterday morning.

'Let us buy a comb, some soap, and a nail-brush,' said Jean. 'Then we can . . .' and we painted delicious pictures of those three hours. We raced across the square at the top of the steps, pausing a minute to gaze at the cabmen gathered about up there. They all sported bell-topper hats. Around us was a babble of Italian. It was the busiest time of the day. Crowds of people were pouring out of the trains below, or rushing into them. We yielded to the spell of this vivacious foreign 'come and go', and nearly danced into the hairdresser's, where we bought our toilet necessaries, in French, aided by pointing fingers.

Then we ran back, round the corner to the Hotel Aquila. The Englishwoman in the tam-o'-shanter had recommended it. A Frenchman in a fair beard met us inside the door. We gave our orders. A bedroom, hot baths, dinner in half an hour. Oh, but you can't imagine how lovely it was to be *there!*

We turned to go upstairs, two dirty, hungry, hot-headed women twelve thousand miles from home. Jean turned at the angle of the stairs and said to the Frenchman in the hall, 'We have to catch the train at Marseilles tonight, so don't let us be late.'

'Marseilles! No train tonight! Tomorrow morning madam means.'

'No train tonight!'

I looked at Jean. Jean looked at me.

'No train tonight!'

'Oh!' cried Jean. 'Are you sure? There's one at nine, isn't there? Look at your timetable.'

The man looked at the big clock on the hall.

'It has just gone,' he said. 'Half past six.'

The minute hand was at the half-hour then. But Jean was out of the Aquila that same second.

'Run, run,' she cried, 'it might be late, we might *just* catch it.'

Oh, awful moment! But what fine stuff we were made of. We gave up everything. We flew across the square, threw ourselves down the steps, and bumped into a guard blowing a whistle alongside a train.

'Marseilles? Marseilles?'

He opened a 'Marsiglia' door and tossed us in. The train moved. We were off.

Oh, miserable moment! Oh, miserable us! Everything just in our grasp, then everything snatched away. I was so angry with Jean. Jean was so annoyed with me. Each felt as if the other had thrown her dinner out of the window. Does this sound very greedy? Oh, but we *were* so faint, so tired! And here we were again, sitting bolt upright with dirty hands and faces, a long night before us, and not a particle of food between us.

A light broke on me suddenly.

'I see it all,' I said solemnly. 'It was that man's *revenge!* He wanted us to miss our train and miss our boat. Fiend!'

'Demon!'

'He understood every word we said. He meant to pay me out for that piece of paper.'

'We may miss it yet,' said Jean, gloomily. 'Alfred will be *frightfully* angry! And what are we to do if it's gone?'

'I don't know!'

I didn't care either.

I believe we would both have rather missed it, and had that dinner at the Aquila, than gone without dinner and caught our boat. You can't imagine how aggravated we were. We were like two hornets, baffled and angry, nearly driven mad.

It was twilight time. A purple mist swathed great Genoa and her lengthened outskirts. Those great, straight houses

with many, many windows and little, narrow, roofless balconies running up, up, up, were like some stage-scene to
us. But an air of squalor, of decay, hovered over the place.
Immense houses and old palaces were shamelessly stained
with damp and dirt. It spread over their sides in great,
brown festers.

Coming straight from Australia, country of plains and
birds and flowers, of lovely colourings, of golden sunlight,
deep skies and vivid waters, if dull in the green of its grass,
Italy was not the exquisite world it might be to one who
comes to it from sober England.

And I began to wonder and wonder. After all, who
knows Australia? Who, of all those who paid homage to
Italy, knows Australia? Not Shelley, Keats, Byron, Dante.
Ah, if they could have dreamed in the blue romance of our
plains and valleys, surrendered themselves to the strange,
warm, golden silence and black shadows, lost themselves
in the infinite poem of the Bush!

Propinquity, love's strongest agent, has been denied
Australia. None of those old great fellows, whose praise
makes a place immortal, have happened to be there.

Never mind, our time will come, is coming.

On, on, through the twilight, through the night. We
could hear the sea lapping on beaches through the dusk.
The rose had faded out of the sky and off the bay. Around
us lay the Italian Riviera. The breaths of millions of flowers were in the air, sweet, heavy, deadening scents. Lilies
and roses, tuberoses and orange blossoms, swept through
the night. It was too dark to see, but we seemed to be in a
world of flowers at the edge of a strange sea.

Then our brains refused to take in anything more. We
fell asleep. I put my purse under my head for a pillow and

lay flat down on one seat, while Jean slept opposite. We must have looked a pathetic pair. The light fell on Jean's face. I looked over at her for a minute. She had actually grown thin round the eyes, and looked so white and so dusty. And yet how adaptable she had proved herself. A thrill of fondness went through me as I watched her accepting our trials so simply and falling to sleep on the dirty seat of a dirty Italian train. I slipped up, bent over her and kissed her. She did not wake. I went to sleep myself then.

At midnight we came to Ventimiglia, and that was the end of Italy.

We had to change trains. We left our carriage, and were carried along in a great stream of Italian peasants coming back from Saturday markets. Men, women and children, laden with bags of vegetables and bundles of all kinds, jostled along with us through the doorways of the station, past the customs men. We were seized with a sense of romance and unreality. It was midnight. We were alone among all these Italians. We, we, *us!* Midnight! Ventimiglia! Sylvia! Jean!

The intoxication of moments like these is what your true traveller must ever seek. Without these moments one might as well stay at home. But with them the world is a glorious place, a delightful, delicious gilt-invitation card to terrestrial and celestial joys.

I daresay Charlie wants to know if we got anything to eat. Yes, we did. We first changed our few Italian coins into French money. Then nothing kept us from that buffet. At a little, round, white table we feasted on sardines and rolls and butter and coffee. They meant new life to us – new life that lasted all the night. We slept no more in the train. There was too much to see and feel. The change into France

66

held us captive. It astonished us. Almost in a moment the whole complexion of things changed. The gloomy, dirty, Italian railway stations, with their slow, dawdling porters, absence of hurry, and unbusinesslike ways, gave place to bright, clean, gleaming stations, spruce officials hurrying to and fro, and crisp language in the air, a suggestion of responsibility understood and accepted, that had been lacking ever since we entered Italy. All was now so quick and gay and clean. The atmosphere was still heavy with sweet flowers, but the odour of decay was gone.

Along the night came a half-arc of light, flaming away miles off, a vivid, flaring arc, the lights of Monaco! Monte Carlo – Monaco.

Our train stopped at Monte Carlo. High up to the right ran white steps steeply. Peering upward we caught gleams of marble in gardens above, and beyond, higher still, a great burst of light from the palace itself.

People came tearing down the steps. Many of them had little bags in their hands. They flew along and hastened into our train, which was soon crowded. Lovely young girls in evening dress and opera wraps, hideous old women, bad old men, faded young men, fast faces, sad faces, mad faces, and many bad faces, all terribly animated, or terribly inanimate.

Our train was full of noise and bustle. It was a corridor train with a long passage going alongside the little compartments. All night long, people were walking up and down. Men were smoking, women laughing, bursts of song and talk and laughter went on without stopping. At some of the stations passengers left us. Towards dawn everyone grew quieter.

Yesterday I had seen the red sun rise over Rome. The day before I had watched a pink and opal dawn break over

Capri and Naples. Today I saw Sol give his first kiss to little gay France, clad brightly in spring green, and I saw her blush an exquisite light blush, fit for an early Sunday morning.

And I thought, 'How happy I am! How lucky!'

Toulon. Aubagne. Marseilles.

It was morning, nearly six. Orchards and orchards had been flying past us. Quaint houses among willows, dear, sweet, little houses, buried deep in vines. This country, too, cried, 'Come back, come back!' I said, 'I will,' for I loved it for its thrift, its cleanliness, its gaiety.

Marseilles, and the real significance of this journey, broke upon us. We were flying to catch our steamer. If we missed it – three shillings between us!

We took a carriage at the station and drove to the *vapeur orientale*. It had been raining here; the streets towards the wharf were dark and slippery. But the buoyant French language kept up our spirits. We had absolutely no idea whether we should find the *Om-er-ac* gone hours before or not due for hours to come. In darkling ignorance one trusts most. We trusted. And as we were trusting, a carriage driving towards us became suddenly alive. Voices shouted. Hats were thrown up in the air. One little man jumped off on to the back step, and thence rolled in the middle of the road.

What was the matter? Who were these people?

Then we recognised them. That was Harry Race picking himself out of the mud. They were parties of fellow passengers leaving the ship for Paris. It was to *us* they were shouting.

More carriages! More huzzas, and waving hands, and tossing hats! It was like a royal reception.

'Bravo! Bravo!' some of them cried. 'Hurry and you'll catch it yet. Goodbye, goodbye. See you in London.'

Our cabby darted on past them and their gay goodbyes. We reached the quay, got into a little steamer, and made off for the big ship in the stream.

Yes. We caught her. There was tremendous excitement as the passengers realised it was the lost ones who were returning at this twelfth minute. Nothing had been talked of since we left but us. We were mobbed, surrounded by people greedy to hear our adventures.

But where was Alfred? Why did he not appear? Someone said that he had wired to the captain that he had gone on to London, and asked him to take care of Mrs and Miss Leighton.

On Jean's berth were two telegrams. One from Naples. One from Rome. Both from Alfred.

> *From Naples*: 'Missed boat. Gone on *via* Paris. Will meet you at Tilbury.'
>
> *And from Rome*: 'Arrived safely here. Take care of yourselves.'

It was dated Rome, eight o'clock. The morning *we* were at Rome. He had travelled up in the same train! If we had only known! Rome, St Peter's, Appian Way, Catacombs, all might have been ours for the asking.

But then we would have missed that journey, that strange, feverish flight through a new world that has already become something infinitely precious, infinitely wonderful, to last me till I die.

What do you think *now* of your

SYLVIA?

CHAPTER V

LONDON, *May* 190—.

DEAR ALL OF YOU,

London! I look back and see myself vainly trying to pierce
the mist and the mystery, to see the city before I come to it;
to realise it as it should be when I came to be in it and of it.
The day came.

It was a surprise from the earliest dawn light. We were
in the Thames, the sky was blue, the light was keen and
merry, and at the water's edge was green grass.

Simple enough that sounds. I now have to look back to
the prehistoric hours before I came to London to find any
cause for surprise in such simple matters. Harking back, I
discover my dream-picture of a boat landing amongst an
overwhelming throng of boats in a dull yellow fog, with a
city rising from the very outside bank in a solid mass of
brick and mortar that would never relent, never yield and
reveal open spaces, never do anything but extend in one
vast, bewildering, shrieking, rattling, roaring mass, till the
brain reeled and the imagination fainted dead away.

Instead, *we* were the only boat. There was no fog, but
sunshine and a pale blue sky. There were only a few houses

visible, and a couple of hotels. And there was grass and a broken bottle or so, and some empty jam tins scattered here and there promiscuously on the grass, as if to say, 'The world's the world all the world over.'

Our ship came up to a wharf, a dirty wooden wharf with dirty wooden sheds. A common, wooden gangway went down. People put their feet on the common gangway and walked down – just a common walk. And there was England. It was all quite common.

Then into the sheds to find luggage labelled and muddled under the letter X, just as it might be muddled anywhere. But a large variation on the ordinary order of things when I handed a fat man a penny, as I saw other people do, and got a 'Thank yer, mum' in return. That was the first uncommonness. Yet even it grew less interesting when I came to the tenth man to whom it was necessary to give a penny, and heard my tenth 'Thank you, mum.' The penny acquired a new meaning, however, from those first moments. It left the region of small boyhood and entered the society of big fat men. It became a Something, and now it is an Institution, and I no longer blush to tip a man in uniform even with that unmanly coin. For in England a penny is four farthings and is taken gladly and without a hint of scorn.

I have a dim recollection of a man I gave a shilling to in those early ignorant moments for carrying my smallest bag. He took it without a word. I suppose he couldn't speak for shock, but I am sure there were tears in his eyes if I had only known to look.

We were an hour and forty minutes extricating our luggage from the sheds, finding a customs officer to examine our effects and give us a pass. Then that pass had to be taken to another official, and some money had to be paid for the weight of luggage going in the train to St Pancras, and men had to be found to put the luggage on the train, and the tickets had to be bought, and the train had to be found. There it was, just at the far side of the shed.

We started off at twenty minutes to eleven. It was our first journey in England and we went first class, by the grace of God, as it were, by the custom of our own country, where everyone goes first class. We had a beautiful blue cloth carriage, and a guard with a voice like one of our Governors. His accent was so superb that I felt it an insult to show my ticket to him. But he took it, clipped it, and didn't seem to think himself different from other guards. Afterwards we learned more about that accent.

As I said before, we left Tilbury Docks at twenty to eleven. We arrived in London at half past one – the slowest train journey I ever took in my life. The train started off. Out of the window flew all the heads that could get there. Only one little window was made to open. The side panes were fixtures, against winter blasts, I presume. Later on we found that a hot day in a train or 'bus in England is an indescribable torture. The air becomes so warm and unpleasant that one feels as if one must tear the panes down. In a 'bus one can escape to the top for air. But a train must be endured in all its primitive stuffiness and discomfort in summer for the sake of being less of a discomfort in winter. John P. Robinson, he might have put in an addendum about London also.

Well, our stuffy train moved its slow length along. We crawled through green paddocks. We realised the saying 'far fields are green'. These were much, oh, ever so much, less green than the impossible verdant-tinted things our imagination had pictured away in sun-scorched Australia. These were bright green, true enough. But still they *were* green, and *only* green. They did not scream in wild, unearthly notes, or cut the eyes like a knife with the vividness of their unnatural hue. Some of them even looked a little seared, a little yellow, a little drought-stricken. You did not think that grass could get browned in England? Neither did I. Ah, me! It was only one of the many colonial delusions.

And then, London.

Peggy said to me one day, 'Nobody has ever described exactly coming to London.' For Peg, then, I'll try. 'Tis hard.

A great many houses, and dullest, dingiest, red-brown the predominating note. Nothing decidedly white, or scarlet, or grey. But *not* the forest of houses, the tangled, unending forest of bricks and mortar. I looked out all the time. 'Is this London?' I kept asking.

'Not quite,' Alfred kept saying.

'Isn't *this* London?'

'Well, just about.'

'This – *this* isn't London?'

'Yes, this is London.'

The buildings didn't walk down on us and swallow us up. There wasn't a mighty roar, or an eternal hum that stunned us at the first moment, or a sickening sea of chimney-pots.

There was a big railway station and all the ship's people again. High overhead was a glassed, arched roof, under which trains were allowed to whistle and smoke.

Goodbye, goodbye, goodbye! People rushing at one another, kissing, and shaking hands. Hundreds of cabs driving away, hands waving from within. Away, away, they all go. All the hundreds and hundreds of men, and women, and boys, and girls who have travelled these thousands and thousands of miles with us, day after day, week after week. Away, away, into London. They are swallowed up. They are never seen again. A few only grow into friends. Their friendship has a beauty that is not terrestrial. It began on the water, under the sky. It is sweetened forever by that beginning.

And then we, too, get into cabs, and our luggage goes up on top. Boxes of all sizes are hoisted up there. That strikes us with surprise. We are frightened the roof of the cab may fall in. But Alfred says, 'It's all right, silly women,' and off we drive. Out of the station, into a street. Cabs in hundreds are driving in all directions. Cabs, cabs, cabs. Is the whole world out in a cab? And this is London. It has closed in on us. It has got us. We are driving through it, a clean, neat city, with high, high houses, and flickering trees of the loveliest, tenderest green growing in squares everywhere.

The squares are all railed round with iron rails. In many of them are statues of famous Englishmen. The gay, bright leafage steals through our senses. It is an *intense* surprise to find trees and grass here. To come upon them in this terrible, dreaded city of fogs and everlasting smoke gives one an indescribable feeling, a moment of love and reeling happiness that is nearly akin to pain.

If first impressions are worth anything, these are your
Sylvia's.

CHAPTER VI

LONDON, *June* 190—.

DEAR ALL OF YOU,

London, London, London, London, *London!*

I want to say, straight off, that if I ever marry anyone it will be a London 'busman or cabman. As for the policemen——

Oh, no! They're far too grand for the likes of me! They would be Members of Parliament out in Australia. If you could but see their moustaches, their air of culture. Their mouths are so highly respectable, their manners the most gentle in the world; even if you were in rags they would be adorable to you.

London! London!

Is it possible there are people in the world who take it quietly? Jean and I went out of our minds three days ago, and have continued to stay there ever since. Last night while we were all at a society play called *The Wilderness*, I suddenly looked at Jean, and she suddenly looked at me.

'*We're in London,*' I said to her.

She looked just as surprised as I.

No; we'll never get used to it. We'll never calm down. Never. We couldn't think of such a commonplace thing. You can only come to London once, for the first time. Let us be mad, let us enthuse all we can. After all, it *is* a big sensation to come to London for the first time.

What do I think of London? My very first impression was that it looks so clean. Why do they call it dirty London? Long streets, long terraces of brown houses, grey houses, drab houses, without roofed balconies, packed neatly back along the sidewalks. It is the absence of balcony that gives the streets that quiet, flat, tidy look. Perhaps I should say balcony in our sense of the word, for I have discovered that many houses have little toy-like galleries, so narrow you could scarcely turn round in them, and without roofs, outside their drawing-room windows. It is some time before I can think of those fragile affairs as balconies.

It is true – smile if you will, and believe me at your pleasure – that I have been out alone and got home again. Why, there's nothing to be frightened of. I shall never forget my first few steps alone outside our hotel. (Please remember I told you I was *non compos*.)[10] I don't know what I dreaded, but was so thoroughly imbued with the belief, brought with me from Australia, that it was absolutely impossible to go out alone without losing your way, that I just stood still – and lost it. I turned to get back to the hotel, walked back the few paces I had come, and there was no hotel. I was lost. I had to ask a policeman. He smiled, a serious, gentle, tender, intellectual, protecting policeman's smile, shot *down* on me in the most beautifully caressing way imaginable, and walked along three strides in the opposite direction, and there it

<hr>

[10] From the Latin, *non compos mentis*, meaning 'not sane; out of one's mind'.

was! Since then I've not been out with anything less than Jean – it is just the same as being by myself though, except that we ask two policemen instead of one.

I want to know how do London policemen get their style, and how can they keep it up? But more than that, how do they get their kind hearts? I didn't think there could be so many in one spot.

At first I thought it was all for me, 'cause I'm so nice and they saw I came from Australia. Alas, the belief was soon blighted! They're the same to everyone, even the dirty slum children who haven't had their hair done for six months. A never-ending array of travellers makes no difference to the quality of their wonderful equable manner. I suppose they learn it at a policemen's school.

What a pity a good school like that should be confined to the police!

You'll think I've seen nothing but policemen. You'll be asking me next, 'Where did you go, Johnson?'

Well, something more poetic is Nelson's Monument. Ah!

I don't mind confessing to you that I like it better than anything in London. It is the typical note rung on English beauty, English valour.

I saw him tonight standing away there against a dull rose sunset, and I thought what a beautiful world it is that builds a statue to a sailor, high up at the head of a long, long, brown monument, and lets the sunset flush the sky beyond, and the bells of many churches steal across the evening with their Sunday cadence.

Jean, of course, is buying all London. When we go shopping we always give ourselves away by exclaiming 'How *cheap*!' The prices seem so low. Then the people in the shop pile it on a bit to suit our innocence.

Sometimes I lie down and let all the different Londons sweep over me. There are so many. In that lies the charm, the glory. There's the London of shops and carriages, the bright pink London, the very most up-to-date London, Head Office of the Manufacture of Modernity.

There's the London of Poets, a grey, mysterious, haunted London, full of souls and spirits, and dead people with long hair; the London that holds fame in its hands and tosses it out sometimes in the strangest places; the London where the writers *live*, where the publishers are to be *seen* – the hardest London of all for us to realise.

There's the London of the Elgin Marbles, a white, proud London, standing quietly there between the Central City and the West End, and holding within grey walls the highest triumph in the world.

There's the London that holds Turner,[11] and all great distances, such a blessed London.

There's the London of green young trees and gay window boxes, a merry, playful, pretty London, a most unexpected London to us with our heads full of that old tradition about London, and fog, and smoke.

There's the great big London, all buildings, and streets, and traffic, and suicides, and horrible tragedies. This is the London it doesn't do to think about too much.

There's another London, but I haven't found it yet. It's the London I thought I was coming to.

I lie on my bed and look out of the window at twilight. I love that dim, high sky so far, far away. The grey and the blue in it, and a hushed dull pink, are making pale violets up there. Who would ask London skies to blaze with the gay turquoise that shines upon my sunny country

---

[11] J.M.W. Turner (1775–1851), the celebrated British landscape painter.

overseas? It would be like robing the Helena of Paolo Veronese[12] in pink satin.

Or like clothing the Elgin Iris[13] in yellow brocade.

Oh, no, no, *no!* These vague skies are full of tenderness to their old city. In their dimness they hide her ugliness. For nothing stands out sharp and clear here as in Australia. Often I see nothing at the first moment of looking; then outlines creep, but never leap, towards me. It is often several minutes before it dawns on me that there, quite near me, are houses, churches.

Especially in the country is it so. At first only an impression of green trees, there gradually come to the outer and inner eye dull red buildings among those trees, yellow cornstalks, the spires of churches, and, at last, a whole village.

In our lit, translucent air we see what we look at immediately, or not at all.

The outlines of our trees and townships silhouette themselves clearly against a vivid sky. But here the trees *loom*. The sky seems far behind them, and their outlines are large, and fat, and blurred, and unless a wind is blowing they stand dead still, as if turned to wood. I suppose it's a proper thing for a tree to do. But give me, instead of the heavy 'immemorial elms',[14] a high jagged line of slim black gums cut against a scarlet sky like a frieze thrown up by God to adorn his heaven.

And give me, oh, give me something far off to look at! Already my eyes ache for great distances.

---

[12] A reference to Paolo Veronese's painting, 'The Dream of Saint Helena' (circa 1570).

[13] This refers to one of Edward Thomason's Elgin Marble Medals, 'Iris' (1820), held at the British Museum. The medal depicts a draped female figure.

[14] From Alfred Lord Tennyson's 'The Princess' (1847).

After a lifetime in a country of far stretches, the eyes feel cramped and hungry as they gaze out over this tiny, tidy, tight little England, with its little fields that are no relation to paddocks, its little puddle-holes called brooks, its dear, insignificant creeks called rivers, and its threads of water called streams.

Now I will tell you a great big secret. No one knows it except me and Turner. As he is dead – God bless his memory! – it falls to me to divulge it. And so:

Turner ought to have been born an Australian. The same Turner, same brain, same eye, same hand, same soul, but with Australia to mother him. In his pictures I see his craving for great distances. And there he would have satisfied himself.

Turner in the Blue Mountains looking away up the Kanimbla Valley one winter sunset!

Instead, he had to draw on his imagination, and go to the classics for something large enough to give his soul full play.

I could die happy this minute if I could see one picture of a silent Australian plain as Turner saw it.

And he never saw it, never, never. Poor Turner, poorer Australia, poorest me.

It is the correct thing to say something about pictures in your home mail. Hence the above. I know it's correct because Jean keeps saying to me, as she sits writing to her mother, 'Sylvia, what was that big picture we liked so much?' or 'Who was it painted that picture you know was so celebrated?' I don't think Alfred writes home about pictures. I hope not. I feel that I can't bear anybody else to be as cheeky as I am.

Yours always,

THE GREAT TRAVELLER.

CHAPTER VII

LONDON, *July* 190—.

DEAR EVERYBODY,

It is weeks and weeks since, but today for the first time I fully realised the beauty of that long sea voyage. It came to me as I sat in a tearoom in Regent Street, of all places in the world for a delicate, spiritual thing like that to come to one.

As I sat there drinking tea on the little flower-decked balcony, with the flash and sparkle and roar of Piccadilly in the sunlight below, everything faded away, and I felt the gentle rocking of the great ship.

There could never have been a more beautiful realisation than mine, flashing out of the most contrasting circumstances.

Jean and Alfred had gone to pay a duty visit in Warwickshire, leaving me in the care of a great friend of ours, and a sort of cousin of Alfred's, a Mrs Vosges, a widow. Opposite me sat Mrs Vosges in black, with her delicate little pale face lit up with her usual light gaiety. Then came my nice big Englishman, Mr Gerald Huntley, who has come to London, and called, oh, ever so many times; then Mr Harry M'George, a lazy London man, with

sickeningly beautiful nails, heaps of money, and an aggra-
vatingly good deal of brains.

I resent him having brains, because otherwise I could
despise him for having nails and money.

He sat there staring at me and saying, 'By Jove,
Australia's a long way away' in the silliest, languidest,
drawliest voice you could possibly imagine. Something
like this it sounded, all ups and downs, and drawn-outs,
and cut-offs: 'BjooveAustreeliahsalongweeaweeah.'

'Are you thinking of going there?' said Mrs Vosges.

'If Miss Leighton will give me her promise to introduce
me to a kangaroo,' said he, still staring at me.

But I forgot to answer. I forgot where I was.

Kangaroo – and by a swift leap I was away, away – not
in Australia, but on the deck of the big white ship that had
lain against her shores and carried me here.

And such a longing to be there again came over me
that I couldn't speak. The physical joy of being rocked to
sleep night after night for thirty-five nights turned the
solid land into a desert. I could see the great ocean paddocks, feel again the five weeks lived out of sight of land,
and Whitman's lines[15] came tumbling along my thoughts:

> Oh, to go to sea in a ship,
> To leave this steady, unendurable land,
> To leave the tiresome sameness of the sidewalks and the
> houses,

---

[15] From Walt Whitman's, 'A Song of Joys', published in *Leaves of Grass* (1855).
The correct lines are:
> O, to sail to sea in a ship!
> To leave this steady, unendurable land!
> To leave the tiresome sameness of the streets, the sidewalks and the houses;
> To leave you, O you solid motionless land, and entering a ship,
> To sail, and sail, and sail!

and entering on to a ship to sail – and sail – and sail.

Thirty-five days from dawn till dusk, and all the night-times; thirty-five times going to bed and getting up again; thirty-five mornings, afternoons, evenings, and midnights all alone with the sea.

All the moonrises came back to me. I saw the moon coming up behind us, silvering our long white tail of foam. Until that moment I had never realised the beauty of moonlight on a lonely ocean.

And I saw the sunrise as we came out of the Red Sea that morning in May into the canal across the desert.

And I saw, face to face, my three moments of pure gold – my first sight of the East, my first walking down a street in Naples, my first vision of England.

They are cut into my memory, burnt into my soul. When I am an old woman I shall turn them out of my remembrance-chest, hold them up tenderly to the light, sigh, smile, and grow young and *keen* again. They shall be my talisman.

And I saw a moonlit night and an old fellow with a red face and kind eyes. Poor old doctor! He died on the voyage back. And I thought of his recitation, and wondered if he had found his lost drink, and hoped so.

I got up and looked at a horrid, common, red geranium. English people *cultivate* them. Think of that!

When I came back I hadn't been crying, because the tears didn't get past my nose, but I felt solemn and out of place.

'What is the matter?' said Mrs Vosges. When I didn't answer she said, in a low voice, 'I expect she's homesick.'

I couldn't tell her then I was seasick. They might have taken away the cream cakes, or shown other signs of pitiable obtuseness.

'I never met anyone like you before,' mumbled Harry M'George. 'You are different from every other woman I know.'

At least, I *think* he said that. I am never quite sure what it is he is saying, but it sounded like that. The look he gave me seemed to match such a sentiment – a look full of alarm, almost of fear, as if I were a kangaroo myself.

I would like Mrs Vosges to marry Harry M'George. She is the sort of woman who couldn't like a man without a good exterior, and I think Harry's nails, and his nose, and forehead, and mouth, and bank account, and boots, would suit her admirably.

I believe she likes him too, and that is why she always pairs me off with him to hide her feelings. You will think I am getting horribly worldly-wise, but I cannot help it. I am. I know it.

Compared to Harry M'George, my countrymen are splendid beings. I love the thought of them in their big grey felt hats, with their deep quiet Australian eyes full of plains and snakes and great silences. Even our city men are to be distinguished among Londoners of a like station. Where an Englishman looks wooden and shallow an Australian man looks green and deep.

Pondering over the intangible something, I find it in the eyes. There lies the difference that strikes the onlooker. There is a depth and stillness there that is not to be mistaken for stupidity.

In English country villages I have seen awfully still faces, but the stillness there was dashed with dullness, almost idiocy. Ah, me, how glad I am to sing the song of a young country like Australia, where everything is growing, or to grow!

Alfred took us down into the country in July to see castles – Kenilworth, Warwick and others.

At first it was a painful thing to me to look along the old villages and see the men and women coming towards me. I had to curb myself and not shudder as they passed. Out of every six one was in some way malformed. There came a man who was knock-kneed; here came a woman bent nearly double, yet not with age. There came a poor unfortunate with a great growth on his neck. There came another with one shoulder high up above the other. Here came men and women crooked all to one side or the other. It was terrible to me. Coming from my fair young country it seemed to me that these men and women, whom nobody even turned to glance at, were shouting aloud, 'Decay, decay!'

How the old shambled, how near the earth they all seemed! I hated myself for thinking these thoughts, but once I had begun to think, to go on was inevitable.

Then I began to study the faces that passed me in the street. Day after day I went about among them, forcing myself to observe.

And I could see after a time that nature was playing strange freaks. She was writing herself on these faces. Not the delicate language of flowers and sunsets, of trees and wind and rain. No. Her imprint was of her lower nature. It was her turnips and carrots, her potatoes and her radishes that she was reproducing in these countenances.

I shut my eyes and see before me the face of an old man. He has two brown knobs for cheeks, a round, protruding knob for a nose, a smaller knob for chin, a succession of knobs for a forehead, all a dusty earthy colour like his earth-coloured velveteen coat. If he is not a potato, what is? So like is he that I am mad some days to take a knife and cut off those little knobs, and peel him and put him in water, which would surely kill him, even without the knife, for, like most potatoes, he does not wash.

Another man I know well by sight is like a carrot. Instead of growing brown and knobby he is long, red and coarse. His chin is like the heavy end of the carrot, and his nose is another carrot, a short, thick one. Even his eyes are like carrots. His hair has nothing to do with the resemblance, being neither green nor red, but the expression of that man betrays beyond all doubt what vegetable he represents. Of all stupid vegetables a carrot is the densest and dullest. Without boiled beef, what is it? This man is an admirable representative. He could sit alongside boiled salt beef for days without spoiling the picture, but put him beside a toasted quail or a grilled chicken and feel the unspoken anguish of those exalted birds at being brought into contact with this earthy product.

And does his wife know he is a carrot? What does it matter to her if he is? She herself is an enormous overgrown beetroot. To us she is a new and unpleasant discovery. We have nothing to match her in Australia. Her big red face and big red chin, and big red ears and big red hands, and enormous body, swaying along the street in a black bonnet and frock, are like a beet dressed up to frighten a child. She makes me feel I will never be friends again with beetroot.

But this is dull, and I am dull, and you are dull, so

AU REVOIR.

CHAPTER VIII

LONDON, *August* 190—.

DEAREST KIT,

Am I homesick? What is it like?

Homesickness is a little like seasickness. I know both.

In homesickness you are walking along a strange place, when suddenly you are rocked back, your brain reels, your senses shrink, you shut your eyes. The sight of these buildings, these trees, these streets makes your head go round. You dare not look at them. A glance, and the ground seems to go from under your feet. You swirl, and seem to be quite empty inside. The disease attacks you without a moment's warning. Its only preliminary symptom is a feeling of fear. You draw back, you know not why, and hate and dread the look of everything around you. You are overcome with a dull distaste for everything in the world. The streets seem to menace you. The loveliest scenery mocks you. The song of a lark, or a thrush, stabs you like a neuralgic pain. The children playing about under your eyes are loathly little objects. All the men and women who pass by you reveal the innate cruelty of all men and women. As for music, pictures, statues – to look at them would be like watching the sea-line float up and down outside your porthole till your cheeks were green. But cruellest of all is the sky over your head. One glance at it and you are undone forever. All you can do is hasten indoors quickly, pull down the blinds, darken your room, and lay your head on your pillow till the awful attack goes by.

You will know you are better when you can see a strange house again without turning white without and a dull red fire within.

To know the incomprehensibly intimate connection between the psychic and the physical, you must, you absolutely must, go through an attack of this kind.

But it's a disease that will not bear too much discussion from the patient.

So farewell, from this your purling stream of silver.

CHAPTER IX

England, *Autumn* 190—.

MY DEAR PEOPLE,

It is autumn, my first autumn. How strange to live to twenty-one and never see an autumn! And how good! It is one of the best things in the world to be twenty-one when you first see the world paint itself red, even if the time that comes after is as melancholy as all times that follow all painting-reds.

Year after year our Bush stands in its grey-greenness. Come winter, come summer, come the fierce wild rains of April, May, or June, come the hot dry winds of midsummer, the summer thunderstorms, the September gales, there she stands proudly, gathering her leaves about her, heedless of the coming and going of the seasons.

Month after month melts into another month. Spring glides into colder weather. Then our little winter says she has come. The sun shines all her time perhaps, shedding a light pure gold from half past six till after five in the evening, and we light our fires, and sometimes we think we are very cold. But, hey presto! Before the cold has time to settle in us it is gone, and the wattle is breaking.

And all the time our gardens are full of flowers, our trees are green with leaf.

I often smile over here as I think of a garden we used to despise so – over there. It was a big, long garden in a suburb near Sydney. All round it was a paling fence. And over the palings flaunted, all the year round, the brightest, biggest, scarletest geraniums. We could see it half a mile away, that great, gleaming hedge. It was like a high broad wall of scarlet. Truly, it was beautiful. But we hated it because – my pen falters with fear as I write it in English ink on English paper – *because it was made of geraniums!*

And here I trot round after people into their conservatories, and stand up before little pots, and say 'Oh!' and 'Ah!' and listen to the genealogy of that pink thing, and hearken how that red creature first cut his teeth, and when he first said 'googul', and wonder if I can be I, and these can be *geraniums!*

So we pay in our old age for the scorn and wickedness of our youth.

In my time I have thrown many a geranium over a fence. As for you, Kit, the piles of black-eyed Susans you have rooted up and tossed into the wheelbarrow or out into the road will rise and haunt you some day, sure as sure. If ever you are taken round English glasshouses and see those black eyes gleaming at you out of Susan's crimson velvet leaves, how you will – laugh?

But autumn, autumn, English autumn, how did I ever live without it? How did I ever live without a pine wood? Oh, my dear gums, you would forgive me if you knew. It is because I loved you so, knew you so, was your dearest, closest friend all the years, and learned all the sweet tree-things from your lips that I love these cousins of yours overseas.

As long as I live I shall never forget the first time I went into a pine wood.

It was three o'clock in an afternoon in October. Gerald Huntley and I were roaming along a country road, crimson with a fire of elm and beech trees. We came to the edge of a pine wood. It belonged to an old castle. I looked over the low stone wall between me and the wood. I could not help myself, I had to cross it. I made him go on alone. I climbed it, and jumped. A couple of blackbirds rose from the grass and scurried away upwards, and I entered my big, wide wood.

Then I knew I had been waiting for this for many years. It closed round me. Is there anything in nature that so tenderly and utterly welcomes and embraces one as a pine wood? Perhaps because as soon as you enter it you can see far, far away, into its very heart.

The instant I came to it, it enveloped me. The world faded away. I was no longer in a wood, among trees, under a sky. I was in a great cathedral, lovelier than any on earth.

A pale, yellow light shone up from the ground. Away, away through the wood, this dull gold floor lay, not shining, but sending up a warm radiance. Millions of goldbrown needles had dropped to the grass till all its green was hidden, till there was no ground, no grass, nothing to be walked on but this warm, wonderful floor. Under foot it was darker, it was nearly brown. But, away up the hillside, under the far trees, it was purest, palest gold. And sometimes, over the gold, there had rushed up scarlet fungi. Whole families gathered near each other in gay patches.

And sometimes there crept through the needles the tiniest, sweetest things in the whole world, little growths with slim, mouse-coloured bodies like violet stalks, and big mouse-coloured hats that drooped and shaded them all round. There was a note of dull mauve in their mouse-colour, and again and again I thought I had come on violets, leafless violets, starring my yellow floors. They were so slight, so fragile, so quaint, so plucky, standing there all alone in the heart of the wood, in their big, little hats, that a story of Tourgueneff's came back to me, an irrelevant story about birds and a hawk. It was the end of the story that my small things stirred in me, the words that the sight of the little birds, fearless of the hawk, stirred in Tourgueneff, '*We will fight on and damn it all.*'[16]

'Fight what?' you will say. Well, whatever comes along to be fought, my dears. You need not look for anything.

Ah, my pine wood, how very good you were to me! You told me all about yourself at once. There were no hesitations, no embarrassments. I loved my wood, my wood loved me. I had not to wait till I knew you. I knew you at once. I loved you at once. And (whisper, whisper, pine wood) it is not so with my gums over sea. Nobody loves them till he knows them, and nobody knows them at once. They are strange, shy, silent things, and will only speak to those who have known them all their lives. They grow sullen with strangers. The few tourists who come so far gaze at them blankly. They say, 'Why, all these trees are *alike*! All Australia is covered with them. Oh, how monotonous! How dull! How melancholy!' And, to themselves, 'How *ugly*!' Perhaps they are ugly. Who is to say?

[16] From Ivan Turgenev's poem 'We Will Still Fight On', in *Dream Tales and Prose Poems* (English edition 1897).

I remember sitting one morning on the verandah of Coolloolloo, and, looking away before me, was filled with the strange beauty of the country. A young Englishman staying there came along and sat beside me. He too looked out, as I was looking. His eyes never softened. Presently he said to me, 'By Jove, how *fearfully* ugly this place is!'

I remember what a shock his words gave me. He went on looking out over the land and seemed to shudder at the sight.

'That black scrub on the hills, that yellow grass on the paddocks, those beastly gum trees, that glaring sky.'

That was what *he* said, and they were what he saw. And as I looked, for one second I almost saw them as he saw them. I suppose I came under the influence of his dislike. Then my old vision flashed back to me. Dear black scrub, dear parched paddocks, dear ghostly gum trees, dear turquoise sky. *I* put the 'dear' to them all that he left out. That was the difference in our way of looking at them. But *what* a difference!

Is it the light in a pine wood that makes all so beautiful?

Yellow lights rise from the ground. Down through the treetops come paler bursts of yellow. You could believe that the sun was always in the same place, always sloping softly down the sky.

Yet these lights have nothing to do with the sun. All the dim glory comes from the pines themselves. The gold below creeps from the fallen gold-brown needles on the ground. The gold above is the massing together of pallid treetops, shading upward into feathery creams and primrose. As you look up it seems as if a setting sun had caught the trees and was sending long shafts of fire along them.

And perhaps there is no sun in the sky that day. Perhaps the grey clouds and mist veil all the light and colour up there. Perhaps the day is leaden and dark. But still the pines shine on. Still the yellow radiance is there, above and below.

I want to know why the world goes to church in a church when it can go in a pine wood? What a silly race to ignore this most perfect place of worship and crowd through doors into buildings! Here there is everything to aid the soul to soar; silence, full of God and the things he made with his own hands; a dim, religious light filtering through nature's own stained windows; a floor of gold and most soft to kneel on; and a spirit, a spirit, a spirit, a gentle, wandering, fragrant spirit, the spirit of the pine trees, surely the gentlest, tenderest of all the spirits of all the forests.

Coming over the world by sea I learnt the meaning of blue and green. Here I have learnt what red is. The deepest meanings to everything are to be found in nature. Red, my dear, colourblind chicks, is not *red*.

It is an incomprehensible force. If we only understood it, and knew how to make colour one of the first forces in our affairs, we might rise high. Alas! how little we know how to apply it to politics and state affairs, or to our inner lives.

People who spend all their lives among these deep colourings grow callous towards them, except when their vanity in their country is aroused. This world wants moving about. There was never a greater fallacy than that old Bible theory about the efficacy of staying in one place all one's life.

Listen to me!

If I had a vote in the affairs of worlds I would shift this whole universe about every ten years with a long pole.

I would warm up the chilly English in wild Westralia, and send the gay French to sober Tasmania. Australians should be shipped to Russia, Russians ought to be sent to Queensland; the Irish might learn to be neat in Holland, and Spain and Norway could make an advantageous exchange of residence. India should be peopled by Yankees. I would send the Greeks to Japan, and the Germans to China, and the Italians to the United States – and in a hundred years what a world there would be, wouldn't there? The world would be everyone's province, and that sickly weed, the Country Family, would be choked out of existence, and that false prejudice called Patriotism would stand exposed.

How we should forge ahead, each nation bursting with the spirit of a new country! Exuberance would take the place of patience, and would carry us forward doubly quickly.

Perhaps!

And here I am in a lone land, with you all far away, and unable, however willing, to migrate hither for many a ten years to come.

Oh, if you could see a red hillside, planted with red dripping trees, standing up against a red sunset. That sight makes you feel that all beautiful things are possible.

It is not alone the physical miracle of a great, green, living wood changing into broad scarlet, changing without the aid of death, the artist who changes all things easily. A deeper thrill than that goes through the senses. If trees that were bare once can deepen and glow, why not souls? If the glow passes from the soul as it dies out of the tree, why may it not come again to the soul as it will come again to the tree?

Out of the autumn, as out of the sunset, I garner faith in an endless succession of dawns in my little, dark, bare soul.

But – such is the passion of a human being for her own land – I found a reason why we Australians should be glad our trees never turn the world over there to orange and crimson, scarlet, blood-red, gamboge.

After the autumn fire has burnt the leaves their deepest and loveliest, comes a terrible time for these English trees. Their spiritual grace deserts them; they stand in base materialism for days and days.

Their leaves turn hard, and dry, and wooden. The red is there, but the life has gone out of it. It is a dead, hard, brown-red. A horrible suggestion of *wood* emanates from the still, stiff creatures. They seem to represent sideboards, chiffoniers, tables, chairs, doors, and ceilings. *Our* trees are saved that awful time. Oh, my country! The indignity of suggesting sideboards is spared your slim, ethereal gums. If they never reach the great glory of these reddened elms and beeches, they never sink to a resemblance to a thing that holds cruets, and tumblers.

Oh, my trees, my trees, stretching on and on, and on, and on, don't believe me when I talk of pines and larches. They are beautiful; the poets loved them. But you! I love you because the poets would have loved you had they known you – and they never knew you, never loved you.

As I came through Italy I thought of all who had loved that land. And then the thought followed that they would have loved my land too had they known it.

Oh, my trees, my land, let me love you passionately till I die! And make up a little for Shelley and Keats and Wordsworth and all the others, whose love and adoration might have been yours had fate been different.

Trees of mine, ah, the nights I listen,
Nights I steal through your black, black shade!
I and the old gums sorrow alone,
The young gums give me their accolade,
Mile on mile through the death-grey silence,
Twilight, midnight, or yellow noon,
And 'tis I who know that your desolate story
Has its hidden sweet and its inner glory.

Dark and Dawn through the grey gums sweeping,
Blazing gold of the Afternoon,
All have revealed the soul of their song,
But where, oh land, is my promised tune?
I am silent, I have no music,
Maestoso nor Allegro.
But you know how fain is my impotent story
To unfold the theme of your veiled, great glory,

And now, my dear people – I nearly wrote 'dear trees', though 'dear sticks' would be more fitting to you after as-similating this tremendously wooden epistle – farewell and goodbye, and forgive my rhapsodies.

SYLVIA.

CHAPTER X

LONDON, *October* 190—.

MY POOR, DEAR FAMILY,

I feel you have been frightfully bored lately. Have you not? And by Sylvia, one of your own. And whatever else we let each other do to each other, we never let each other bore each other.

So no more trees, no more caprices, no more sentiments; nothing now but life, life, life!

I wish I could write you something very funny. I want to be making you laugh instead of yawn. What can I tell you? Let me think.

I think, and think, and think. Nothing comes. Truth to tell, there's nothing very funny over this side of the world. Everyone goes several degrees softlier, sadlier, than we do. They don't laugh as quickly, talk as easily, or feel the pulse of the world as keenly.

We go out a great deal. Alfred's people have handles to their names, and Jean says she opens their doors more easily – feels in her element with them. But I miss the glad Australian spirit of the city, and the sad Australian spirit of the Bush. It seems to me that girls and women over here rarely sparkle. In conversation they rather sit on their talk than rise up with it. Are we a naturally giddy and plea-sure-loving country, I wonder? The gaiety and verve we put into our accounts of things, as we tell them to each other, is lacking in this frostbitten island.

Strange, by the way, that such a dolorous literature should emanate from such a light-hearted people as we are.

Speaking of literature, here is something for you, Peg. We met a famous publisher the other day at a dinner in Bohemia. Said he to me, 'You come from Australia, I believe.'

Said I to him, 'Yairs.'

(Say you, 'Not much verve in *that*.')

Said he, 'I believe you have a wonderful climate over there. What I mean to say is, from what I can gather, it seems so clear and fruity.'

I said it was a peculiar climate (I was not going to give away our climate to a publisher, who might have bound it up without gilt edges and sent it to a reviewer to be cut and dried still more dry).

Said he – true as true – 'What is the ordinary clothing of men out there? What I mean to say is, what do they wear?'

I thought of answering coats, and hats, and trousers; but while I paused, with the natural shrinking of a woman from mentioning these garments, he continued, 'I hear men give as much as thirty pounds for their hats.'

This is one of the times when you feel your miser-able ignorance of your native land. This man seemed to know things I had never learnt of. I had an idea that I *had* heard of someone giving a lot of money for something in Australia, but I thought it was a racehorse. Here was this smart London publisher telling me it was a *hat*. I was ashamed to show how little I knew of my own race, and meanly fenced by asking him which of the minor prophets wore the biggest hat. Heaven only knows why I asked him that! The Bible itself throws no light on the subject. After a little consideration, he gave it up, and I had to answer my question myself. The answer was, 'The one who had the biggest head.' By the time he had tried to laugh, and failed, I hoped he had forgotten the hat that cost thirty pounds. Not at all. He returned to it at once, and although I mumblingly remarked that any man might pay that if his hat was big enough, I could see what an ignorant creature this man considered me.

'Perhaps it was twenty pounds,' mused he. 'What sort of a hat do you think would it be?'

'How much does a pee-wee cost?' I asked.

'Pee-wee? Is that a bird?'

'A hat – we are talking of hats.'

'A pee-wee hat! Is that an Australian manufacture?'

'Not at all! I have seen lots of them in England.'

Oh, dear. For then I had to enter into a description of pee-wee hats, as if I wasn't punished enough for being a 'girl from Australia'.

'Little brown hard things, sometimes black,' I lucidly explained.

'Hard-hitters!' said he, enlightened. 'Oh, no, no, no. I assure you it wasn't a hard-hitter. What I mean to say is that men out in your colonies wear big slouch hats, sometimes of felt and sometimes of straw. Would it be a felt hat or straw hat that cost so much?'

'Possibly a cabbage-tree.'

'And do they really go up to such prices?'

(Mother, why didn't you have me taught everything about drapery, so that I could converse with men who follow intellectual pursuits?)

'I really don't know.'

It was time I made that answer. I should, in truth, have resorted to it long before, but who cares to show that she doesn't know everything about her own country – and a bit over – when a long way from it?

'I believe it *was* a cabbage-tree hat. What I mean to say is, what is the ordinary price of them? Why are they so expensive in Australia?'

'I really don't know.'

('What a terrible waste of opportunities!' Peg is thinking.)

'I suppose your climate prevents men from dressing exactly as we do. What I mean to say is, they do not wear such thick clothes, I suppose, as we do? Do they wear waistcoats?'

You would think it was the easiest thing in the world to answer these simple little questions; but there descended on me suddenly the awful responsibility of telling the exact truth about the manners and customs of my countrymen, and at the same time there flashed all over me an inclination to embroider – not particularly the garments in question, but as many of the facts relating to Australia as lay in my possession. Everyone who has travelled in strange lands will understand.

It is a temptation that assails women as well as men. Even people like myself, who never shot or caught anything, are overcome with the desire to 'draw the long bow'.

I paused, hesitated, and was lost. There seemed something so tame in the fact that my countrymen *did* wear waistcoats. I thought to myself he would think to himself what was the use of living all those thousands of miles away from London tailors if you didn't go without a waistcoat? And I said as follows, 'When they don't wear waistcoats, they wear their cummerbunds.'

His eyes showed a new interest. I saw at once *that* was what he wanted. I was right when I thought he would have thought it a terrible waste of space to live all that way off and wear a waistcoat. In a pleased voice he said, 'Cummerbund! What is that? What I mean to say is, what *is* a cummerbund?'

'A sort of man's sash, worn round the top of the waist.'

'Oh, I see. What colour?'

'Red, sometimes.'

'Oh, I see. How jollay!'

I continued to be interesting to him, and then we got to a subject of which I am heartily sick – Australia and the War. Between ourselves, one hears of Australia only in two conjunctions here. With cricket. With the War. As a nation of men and women, thinkers, workers, po-ets, dreamers, idealists, pantheists, writers, labourers on the land, we don't exist. All England thinks of us can be summed up in half-a-dozen words:

'*You were so good to us in the War.*'

My dears, if I have heard that once I've heard it a hun-dred times. In London, in the country, in little villages and big towns, those words have been tossed towards me:

'*You were so good to us in the War.*'

Yes. It's a sad, mad truth, hard for us to swallow. England never gave us a thought before. She doesn't pretend oth-erwise now. With a delightful calm, and a funny absence of tact, she casts round for something nice – or otherwise, as long as it's something – and finds she thinks nothing but that:

'*You were so good to us in the War.*'

I confess I hear it with a flare of irritation. Of course, of course, we appreciate their gratitude – of course, of course, of course. But is that all we've ever been – is that the final significance of our land – to be good to England in a war?

And here at this dinner, those fatal words again, not for the first time tonight. They accompany every introduction where the word 'Australian' is pronounced.

And everyone says it so seriously. Oh, so profoundly seriously. You couldn't possibly laugh; you'd die if you did, sooner or later.

And after the War, what did we speak of then?

Still of Australia. My companion persisted. He wanted to know if the bushmen were black. But gradually there stole over me a juster frame of mind. After all, after all, why should it ruffle me, this ignorance of England about us, eating our hearts out to come to her, calling her always 'Home'? What does it matter? How could it well be otherwise? We are so far away. We have no literature that she knows or cares to read. We have no way of attracting her attention over all those seas and oceans. Why should we want it? That is what puzzles us all when we are *here*. Will the day come soon when we learn to put on our own hallmarks? To be content without the approval of England, to live and die for our own country and call Australia 'Home' and England 'England'?

I say '*soon*', because it must come, is coming, even now.

SYLVIA.

CHAPTER XI

LONDON, *November* 190—.

DEAR EVERYBODY,

One, two, three, four, five! At the top of the fifth, there you are. This is where I 'hang out'. Here's my Temple of the Muses. Back room, fifth storey, up near a London sky. Enter.

'I want nothing else in the world,' I said the other day, ecstatically.

'You don't want much then,' said Jean. She didn't mean to be sneering. She simply didn't understand.

How was she to know in that 'little back room in Bloomsbury', with a big elm blown against the window, and far below a long green garden walled round with a high brown wall, Heaven itself could be had for the asking, and often came without an invitation?

It isn't a little room either. It is huge, immense. It stretches thousands and thousands of miles. It holds within it golden Australia, Rome, Naples, Genoa, the Mediterranean, the desert, Port Said, the Darling Downs, the dear yellow Thames, wrapped in its dull haze, Kandy with its soft outlines, the bleak, desolate, brown, pointed hills of the sad Arabian coast, Westminster and the Poets' Corner, a grove of gum trees in Civitavecchia, the green sunlit hills and vineyards of Sicily – a wonderful, illimitable world of sea and land and sky.

Jean and Alfred have gone to the Continent. I am alone for the winter.

I have begun my music lessons. Emmie Jones, who has been here three months, has the room next to mine. We share a little piano, for which we pay one-and-three a week each. We pay thirty shillings a week for our board. We pay a shilling a week for our gas. We pay eightpence for every scuttle of coals, and sixpence for every bath. Now you know all our secrets. Our rooms are big enough to turn round in, with care. But what do *we* care? London is outside the window, and so is the elm. We are living out a dream – the dream of every Australian girl. Other people may be happy, but nobody else in London is happy with the same superlative, mad, glad, wide, deep, shimmering, sparkling, irrepressible, causeless happiness that dances all day in our veins.

Imagine a wide brown street, shadowed softly with violet mist and fog.

On either side, from end to end, are tall brown houses. They have no balconies. They make one long line of brown, so straight you want to lay a pole along it and *feel* the flatness.

At each end of the street is a little square, with a black iron rail round it, and an iron gate. The gate has keys, but only people living round the square are allowed to use them. We are not opposite a square, so we cannot go in there and lie on the grass, or sit under the bare black trees. Our house is just at the corner, too, but they will not let us share. In winter it is no deprivation, but yet it is good to be able to look through the open rails and see the grass, and feed the eye with a little greenness in the midst of a brown forest of houses. Charles James Fox stands at the other end of the street, just inside the rails of a square. His statue is brown and dirty, but I like to have him so near.

'I love my boarding house,' I wrote to Jean in Paris. 'If you love *me*,' Jean wrote back, 'make it *Pension*.'

So I made it *Pension*, and *Pension* it is.

Our house is like every other in the row. Window after window, storey after storey, stair after stair. The higher you get the cheaper you are, till you get to heaven at thirty shillings a week. It is a typical London boarding house – I beg its pardon, I mean *Pension*. We have eggs and bacon and fish for breakfast every morning of our lives. So do all the other *Pensions*. We dine at seven. So do all the other *Pensions*. The simultaneous boom and rattle of their gongs fill the street like a cavalry charge three times a day. Then on Sunday night we have a very English institution – nine o'clock supper – a high tea which takes the place of dinner and leaves people free to go to church.

A boarding house in Bloomsbury!

To some people, no doubt, these words are provocative of horror and dismay.

To us they mean freedom, life, novelty, fascination, everything that makes the days worth living.

Bloomsbury! Is there not something intensely magnificent in the word? We think of all the great people who lived there. That brown house at the corner of Bloomsbury Square, shall we ever come to pass it without looking, as other people do? That was Disraeli's house, a stone's throw from us. I wake in the night and think how wonderful and rich I am to live so near him, to be able to look at his house every day.

And in the next square to the west Christina Rossetti lived and died.

One day I received a rude shock. Mrs de Burg and Ellie, who have been in London two years now, came to see me.

'*Of course* you are not going to stay here?' said Mrs de Burg.

'For the winter.'

'But not here, in this neighbourhood?'

'Certainly, I am not thinking of moving.'

'But it isn't a *good address*,' with a most pronounced emphasis.

'A good address? Why, it is the most convenient part of London.'

'But it isn't a good address to *give*.'

'Why, Disraeli used to live here.'

Mrs de Burg looked at Ellie and Ellie looked at her and they both burst out laughing. They were evidently very much amused.

'I believe she thinks it's a place to be proud of living in,' said Ellie.

'I hastened to tell my people I was in Bloomsbury so that they could be as proud as I am.'

They laughed again. Then Mrs de Burg grew serious.

'My dear,' with the new staccato voice, quite different from the old soft Sydney drawl, 'you don't understand. I don't say anything about what Bloomsbury *was*. I am talking about what it *is*. It may have been fashionable once, but since then everyone has moved west.'

'Why, this is west – West Central.'

'Ah, but it is the "Central" that does it. That "C" makes all the difference. You *must* have "W" by itself in your address. If you have to write "C" after it, you're nobody. You're almost east.'

'Do you mean to tell me people move away from these comfortable quarters just to have "West" alone in their address?'

'It makes *all* the difference.'

'Well, then, I refuse to be driven away from a place by any letter in the alphabet from A to Z.'

Mrs de Burg sighed impatiently.

'You silly child! Well, you will have to find out for yourself that what I say is true. Netta Raymond, Mary Cobbe, Ethel Mapleson – they all came here first and *had* to go west afterwards to get away from that "Central".'

'When I went to see about my art lessons,' said Ellie, 'I gave my address as it was then, Torrington Square, Bloomsbury. "Why do all you Australians and Americans go to the West Central district?" asked my instructor.'

'We were only here a few weeks,' explained Mrs de Burg. 'We found it an *impossible* address.'

'It is good enough for Mr and Mrs Theatre-Brownes, for the famous Mr Jonas Scrabbe, and other well-known people. They all live round here.'

Mrs de Burg crushed me with an extraordinary assertion.

'They *live* here, my dear. That makes all the difference.'

'But I *live* here too,' said I.

'Oh, no, you only stay at a boarding house.'

'Oh, but I assure you I live. Rather! I very, very, *very* much live. Far more than at Potts Point or Darling Point. Twenty steps and I am in among the Elgin Marbles. Three minutes and I come to the little Rossetti Church with the famous altar painting, and the altar stone to Christina with the words, "Give me the lowest place!" Sometimes I get up in the black morning and go out in the streets before six and roam about the streets and squares. Through the blackness the lamps glimmer dimly. Then the areas begin to wake up. And the glow of fires and gaslights from the kitchens below shines along the streets. The bare black trees and I have the city all to ourselves. From square to square I wander. I watch a yellow wash spread itself softly, palely, over the dark sky. The black trees grow blacker. They sharpen themselves against the yellow. On and on I go. And after a time I find I am not alone. With me are wandering the goodliest company – Thackeray, Beaconsfield——'

'Why, they are dead!' shrieked Mrs de Burg into the midst of my eloquence. I believe she was astounded at my ignorance.

'What do they say to you?' asked Ellie, sarcastically.

'Thackeray says, "Little girl, I've often roamed round here in the dark like you're doing, when I couldn't sleep, or was coming home late from a party. I'm so glad you like the neighbourhood." Have some tea?'

And I plied them with tea and muffins, and they went away heavy-hearted – with me, not with muffins.

When Emmie came home, I told her all about it.

'How funny!' said Emmie. 'Why wasn't I half an hour earlier? Colonials are all the same. They all believe it is the address that does it.'

She had a paper in her hand. She opened it, found a paragraph and read aloud to me: 'There are signs that Bloomsbury is going to be the fashionable quarter again.

Mrs Diamond Spots has taken a house there, and so have Mr and Mrs Mixless Blue.'

'I'll tell Thackeray next time I meet him in the dark,' said I, frivolously.

'They want me to go and leave you,' said I to my elm that night, as I heard her tapping against my window frame. 'They want me to go west – not to follow the sunsets but simply to leave you, my dear, beautiful, haunted Bloomsbury.'

And the elm, the only elm I've ever had all to myself to talk to going to bed and getting up, shivered delicately against my pane. Do you wonder? If anyone else wants me to get a new address, I'll change mine to Sylvia, Care of the Elm, but for the present – I remain,

Yours in deepest Bloomsbury,

SYLVIA.

CHAPTER XII

Dearest all,

After all, I did not tell you much about our *Pension*. Mrs de Burg interrupted. Now I am going to tell you more about a life that will seem very strange to you away over there in the land of homes.

When you think of a London boarding house, you see a landlady in curl papers, and asphyxiate yourself in the odour of onions as you enter the front door.

Our landlady is quite young and pretty. She has smooth dark hair and housekeeps peaceably. Her father and brothers chaperone her. She is a very prim, young, brown-eyed gentlewoman, and sits at the end of the table with an impenetrable dignity that fills us with admiration. She looks about twenty-one, is really good to see, and impresses you with the belief that she is just as good as she looks. She dresses stiffly and simply, and has a stiff little simple laugh to match. Hers is the typical English-girl laugh. It has a little white railing all round it, and never leaps over the railing. It has no gurgle of merriment in it, no gust of spontaneous amusement. I think I may

111

justly describe it as a pretty, sober edition of a giggle, kept all in the front of the mouth – in front of the teeth, in fact. It suggests a pure, good, self-possessed, narrow little soul behind it.

As for the front door, when it opens you are met, not by onions, but by a tall, fair youth in a dress suit, who answers to the name of Carl and hails from Austria. Yes, all day long we are flanked by a German waiter in evening dress. At first this strikes us as superb. We feel inclined to speak of him as 'The Butler'.

Consider it. A tall butler, with a nice face and a foreign accent, in a dress suit, and Disraeli's house just round the corner!

And there are many, many other advantages. There are three American girls, one American professor, an Austrian professor, a French writer, an American actor and his wife, two Cambridge men whose homes are in Germany and Canada, a young Swede, two Australian medical students, and two young men from South America.

Never in my life before have I met an American girl, an Austrian man, an intellectual Frenchman, a Swede or a South American. It is a perfect *embarras de richesses*, this company of varied nationalities.

I am glad the Swede and the Austrian can scarcely speak a word of English. The rawer, the better. I am glad the South Americans have been only a week in England.

They have all the more of their own countries clinging to them. To me they are incalculably above lords and dukes and duchesses and pearls and rubies. That Swede doesn't know it, but he is a fjord, a Skagerakk and

Kattegat[17]. These South Americans are absolutely uncon-
scious of it, but they are the Rio de la Plata and Buenos
Aires, and a wide, free country something like our own.
The American girls – but stay, I would not dare to say
there is anything *they* do not know. They are probably
quite aware of the strange fact that they are Walden, and
Brooklyn Ferry, and Walt Whitman, and Louisa Alcott,
and the green hills of Vermont where the maple syrup
comes from, all in one.

And all this in one dingy house in Bloomsbury! Do
you wonder that I would not go away? By living here I
live in Sweden, on the Danube, all over the States, in Paris,
through South America, all at the same time. It is intoxication. It is Life – capital 'L'.

The three American girls sit opposite us at breakfast and
dinner. Their names are Estrella, Cynthia and Gertrude
Hawkins. We are the first Australian girls they have ever
met, and they are our first Americans, so our mutual interest in each other is lively, and manifests itself in eager
conversations across the table, and, as we get to know each
other better, in our bedrooms at night.

To look at, they are sallow, thin-faced girls, saved from
extreme plainness by the splendid pose of their heads and
the fine carriage of their shoulders. They have straight
dark hair brushed up loosely in front and very tightly at
the back. When they speak they always seem to be saying,
'Yang', and they all 'yang' away together, interrupting and
contradicting each other, as if one 'yang' was not enough
at a time.

In my extreme ignorance I came here believing that
there was no accent in the world so ugly as what we call

[17] A Norwegian strait: the Kattegat is a sea that lies to its south.

the 'Colonial'. But when I heard the voices of Estrella, Cynthia and Gertrude, who had travelled all round Europe, and been two years in Paris, I came to the conclusion that London must in justice allow our accent to escape scot-free while chaining up such terrible inflections as theirs.

The American art student, with a head like a coconut and a firm, thin mouth, has not so much of an accent, but he has a queer method of arranging his emphasis. He says, 'And she *was*.' (Then I think he has finished.) '*The*.' (Then I am sure he must have finished.) 'Most awfully stunning girl.' (Then, and not till then, he *has* finished.)

I cannot always understand what he says. The other day, describing a girl to me, he said, 'She was vurry Doric.'

Doric! my thoughts leapt to Greece, and I thought what a poetic mind he had. I tried to catch his exact meaning.

'Much Doric-er than Miss Jones,' he added.

Emmie! Was *Emmie* Doric? Then suddenly, just in time to save the question on my lips, I saw how he spelt Doric – *D-a-r-k*.

'The King and Queen don't look in the least hotty,' says Cynthia to me one day.

I wonder what on earth she means. Hotty? What is 'hotty'? I puzzled over that for days. At last, I got a piece of paper and a pencil, and said to Cynthia, 'I want you to write down a little sentence for me – "The King and the Queen don't look hotty."' I gabbled it off quickly, so she would not detect anything incongruous in my pronunciation of the baffling words. She wrote: 'The king and the queen don't look haughty.'

'My!' said she, 'I believe you are after my autograph. It is *Estrella*, not me. I guess you have made a mistake.'

'Is Estrella very famous?' I asked tentatively.

'I guess she will be, when she gets back to the States. I'll show you a photograph of her Salon picture.'

So I discovered that Estrella, the youngest of the three, had had a picture in that year's Salon. It seemed a glorious achievement. Had Estrella been an Australian, she would have worn the placard of her picture on her forehead, visibly or invisibly, but Estrella is so occupied with the proud thought that she is American that she has no room for any minor form of pride. She showed me a photograph of her picture – a strong portrait of an old French fishwife.

America must be a wonderful country. I gather from Estrella, Cynthia and Gertrude that there is nothing in the world so big and beautiful that America cannot eclipse it.

Beautiful is not the right word, perhaps. Just to be beautiful would seem to them a poor accomplishment were it not supported with conspicuously superlative qualities. Their lovely landscapes must have the highest mountains, the tallest trees, the bluest skies. Their lovely woman must possess the finest figure and complexion, the largest number of intellectual and social graces. Their flowers – but, now that I come to think of it, they seldom speak of flowers.

As far as America from Greece! There is a new symbol of remoteness for you.

One afternoon Cynthia, Estrella and I went for a walk together in the park. We left home about three o'clock. Out into the violet-misted street we stepped, round Bloomsbury Square, with its dead black trees, down Shaftesbury Avenue, across Trafalgar Square. Then down some steps, and into a great black and grey and violet land, with dim red lights shining down long straight rows of bare black trees – St James's Park.

The air was cold, but not to the skin. It did not spring gaily against the face. It crept in, sneakily in, in to the very bones. That is the difference between English and Australian cold. It always takes me some time here to know whether I am cold or not. I have not grown used to a chill that does not meet the face, but slips into one invisibly, and does not announce its coming till it has settled down into one's marrow.

It was the hour when winter parks are at their best. Four o'clock, and the red sun just dropping away behind Buckingham Palace. Something warm and pink was struggling tenderly with the grey and violet mists.

The pond was frozen over. We stood on the bridge and looked up the glimmering stretch of rose-flushed ice, with its fringe of inky, feathery trees, towards the setting sun.

'I guess they haven't much room here to skate,' said Estrella.

'Why, no,' said Cynthia. 'This isn't half the size of *our* pond. I guess we could hold twenty times as many skaters.'

'My, yes! Our ice is ever so much thicker.'

They discussed the relative merits of skating in the States and skating in England. I could see it was necessary for them to announce that their ice was thicker and their skating lasted longer, but I wished they would wait till the sun had set, and the glow had faded from the frozen lake, and the bare black trees had lost their delicate keen outlines in the blur of the evening.

I was afraid to say anything about that red transparent ball of vivid light. I feared Elfreda[18] would tell of bigger and brighter balls of light over in the States.

---

[18] Previously Estrella: see A Note on the Text.

I will believe all she tells me about the thickness of her ice, and the number of her skaters, but when it comes to suns I will hold my own opinions.

For all suns, like all little children and all flowers, are beautiful, none more than any other.

Hundreds of white gulls stood about on the white ice. They made an enthralling study in white. Then the rose from the sky caught them all, and birds and ice were suddenly transfigured. It was like Fairyland come true, the rose and white sheet of frozen waters, the pink-flushed birds, moving a little, or standing in carven stillness in the midst of a white, still world.

'I guess Buckingham Palace isn't much to look at,' said Elfreda, with a loud yang.

'Let us walk round and see it nearer,' said Cynthia.

'Shan't we wait till it gets darker?' said I.

'Why, no, we shouldn't be able to see,' said Elfreda, sensibly.

So they tore me away from the rose-birds on the rose-ice, and we walked on round the pond, and in front of the palace Cynthia declared the architecture did not please her. It was altogether too plain and homely. She suggested several improvements.

If ever Cynthia marries – as every good American girl hopes to marry – a prince or a duke, she will make a great stir among the palaces. I can see that her fixed idea is to re-model these stately edifices on the lines of the millionaires' houses in the United States.

'I reckon they are simply out of sight,' said she. Her praise can go no higher. Yes, she means that for praise.

To hear her speak you would think nobody ever lived in a house worth living in but those millionaires of hers. A carriage drove by us. We caught a glimpse of a kid-gloved hand holding a big cigar. It was the King on his way to Marlborough House. I trembled to think what might have happened if he had heard the proposed improvements to his palace.

The sun went right away. The park grew dim and shadowy. Only the long lines of red lights down the side of the wide walk cut the gathering dark. I walked along sullenly. A painful truth was dawning upon me. I suspected it first at sea. Now it began to grow to a certainty. I am an un-Christian, unhuman being. Whenever there is anything beautiful, I want to be alone. I dislike – I almost hate – my race.

It may be that I have not yet had the good fortune to have near me, when the beautiful things are near, someone who would care as I care – absorbingly, forgetting everything else in the world for a while.

But it may be that I am all wrong and other people are all right. And then? Cheerful prospect, life ahead. I'll never marry. If it is so difficult to find the right person with whom to go on a simple walk, or a sea voyage, how impossible it must be to find the right being with whom to travel a whole lifetime.

And the ugly truth flashes on me. This all means I am predestined to be an old maid. This is why I can scarcely endure the voices of Estrella and Cynthia telling about their enormous Statue of Liberty. It must be a great satisfaction to them to be able to reel off the superlative statistics that belong to that statue by right – and misfortune.

At dinner that night Estrella tells Gertrude about our walk.

'We had a good look at Buckingham Palace. It wants painting. We saw the King . . . We passed a shop where you can get our rubbers, and I took the address.'

But not a word about the ice and the birds in the sunset. I ask myself, in surprise, 'What are they to Estrella? Does she care for them ever so little?' No, she was too busy to look at them. Buckingham Palace and its defects engrossed her. When she did glance at the ice, it was only to make a mathematical calculation of how many more people her ice would hold. And yet, she is an artist. She painted that strong portrait. Was Paderewski[19] right when he said American art would produce only portrait painting? When Elfreda goes out, she looks at everything with a hard eye. She takes in every detail of the outside, never ceases to make comparisons, and gives her whole mind to the collection of facts.

They are stuffed with facts, these three Americans. Facts ooze out of every sentence. Day after day they go out fact-hunting. Year after year the search continues. They can reduce the intangible to a fact. They squeeze facts out of Mona Lisa, pick them off the Milan Cathedral, off 'the height, the space, the gloom, the glory', tear them from skies and seas, inhale them and breathe them out, without ceasing. They even try to rend some out of me – poor, factless me. But the operation is not successful. I have forgotten, if I ever knew, what salary our Attorney-General gets, and how many inhabitants there are in West Australia. It is a disgraceful ignorance, but to me there is more than a little joy in owning it.

The darkest ignorance grows fair beside their ubiquitous, unfailing knowledge.

---

[19] Ignacy Jan Paderewski (1860-1941): a successful Polish pianist, composer and politician.

Strange discussions go on round our table. One day it is the Negro Question in the States. How Cynthia, Elfreda and Gertrude overwhelm us with their statistics! Not that they are aggressive, loud or bold. They are simply positive – dead, dead positive. Can a woman be anything worse – at dinner? Another day it is Chinese labour. Other subjects which our *Pension* illuminates with brilliancy over its roast beef and apple tart are international politics, the war in the Transvaal, the new play, London *Pensions,* hurdy-gurdies,[20] food, metaphysics, dress, preachers, manners and customs, and English cooking. How everyone abuses the latter!

Once, someone asks Emmie if damper is good to drink. She struggles to describe what manner of good thing damper is to eat, and how it is made.

'Why, that's hoecake! That's what our coloured people eat,' cried Elfreda; which makes one feel – coloured.

Miss Landegann, at the end of the table, hears some strange things about England. She sits cool and calm through all, and never contradicts or sets anyone right. Her self-possession is really noble. It is a moral lesson to excitable Australian girls like ourselves.

She learns that the English don't know how to cook vegetables; that St Paul's wants painting; that the quickest way to get to Hyde Park is to take a train from Liverpool Street; that you can't get shoes fit to wear in London; an incalculable number of dark insinuations against 'bus guards who will not stop to let people off or in; that it is incorrect to call a nib a nib, that it should be called a pen; that a pie isn't a pie, 'tis a pudding; that cakes are not

---

20 A violin-shaped stringed instrument that produces sound by turning a crank that rubs a wheel against the strings.

cakes, they are biscuits; that biscuits are not biscuits, they are crackers; that English women do not know how to carry themselves; that English women have no idea of dress; that English businessmen are the slowest in the world; that London is wound round and round with red tape that is cutting its throat by degrees; that English bacon is simply 'out of sight'.

Oh, we know a great deal at our *Pension*, I can tell you. We can settle the affairs of nations with a shrug. We can speak ten languages at once.

The nice, clean Swede begins to pick up a little English as time goes on. He is a tall, fair boy, with the clearest blue eyes and merry mouth. For a long time he subsisted on two English expressions, 'Of course,' and 'May I haf?' but now he has added half-a-dozen others. One Sunday night before supper Emmie and I and Cynthia and Gertrude sat chatting by the fire in the drawing room, when the door opened and in walked Mr Young. His name is not Mr Young, by the way, but he has arranged that it shall be, since nobody in the house can pronounce his real patronym. He was just from church. He had on a long black coat and a shiny top hat, and he stood in the doorway and looked at us. Then this apparition announced, with determination and violently pouted lips, and eyes directed at Emmie, 'Want – play – ping – pong.'

Aha! Emmie has cast the spell of her purple eyes over him. It is to her he addresses himself whenever he finds a word to say.

The two South Americans talk Spanish always. They are handsome, tall, slender young men, with dark faces and long waists, and top hats and long coats, always dashing out in cabs, or rushing hastily upstairs with other tall, dark, young men who seem to find the world a lively place, to judge from the talk and laughter they scatter about. I confess I am filled with curiosity about them all. I want to know about them from the very beginning.

But English people do not take much account of Swedes, and Germans, and South Americans, or even Americans for that matter. One afternoon, when Mr Gerald Huntley was calling, he asked me how I liked London now.

'Very much. It's so interesting to know Americans,' said I.

'*Americans*! I don't set much store by *them*,' said he.

I thought how *blasé* and indifferent he was.

But when I thought it over I came to realise that an American could not possibly be the same thing to him as to me. He had probably met hundreds. I had met just these at this house.

He even declared, too, that he did not see anything interesting in Swedes, Germans, Austrians, or French.

'*Interesting!*'

He laughed outright in a way that reminded me of Mrs de Burg when I declared my allegiance to Bloomsbury. He does not regard them as human beings; from the summit of his house at Hyde Park and his stately father and mother, he is able to look down on them as queer things that wear strange garments, have strange, un-English figures, and are of no more importance in the scale of life than flies on a wall. They are not even Kattegats and Skagerakks to him.

There are thousands of them all over London. Is it because they have no homes, no characteristic surroundings, are just merged in the great ebb and flow of life that they are to be considered of so little importance? Heart and brain count for nothing without a house or a background of friends and relations. Poor foreigners! Well, there is someone who takes an interest in you, who weaves pictures of your homes that you had to leave behind you, and surrounds you with them, and gives you mothers and fathers, and brothers and sisters, and social status, and friendships, and all you gave up to come to work in London and be merely a foreigner, a fly on the wall.

On Sunday afternoon dear, beautiful, haunted Bloomsbury is alive with them. Doors open all along the streets to let out strange beings in long coats. In twos and threes I see them pass. Here comes a characteristic group. One man is short and dark. From the back he looks like a coffin. Whether he owes the resemblance to his tailor or his creator I am unable to say, but it is increased by the likeness to undertakers of the two long, dark men on either side of him. They all laugh. The effect is ghastly. Not because it is like a funeral laughing, but because their white teeth and black moustaches seem to curl up all over their cheeks. And here is another group, four this time – four fair-haired, sad, innocent-looking youths in big hats and frock coats, walking as if they made belief they were going to see someone nice, but would find their walk end at their boarding house presently.

As for the Austrian professor with the yellow beard and skin like a baby's, it was he who gave the *Pension* its supreme sensation one night. Unfortunately Gerald Huntley was not there to hear.

But the Americans were.

He came in to dinner in his usual meek and amiable way. He sits at my right, and tells me, in the little English he has, about his great discovery of a simple little fern that predicts fireballs, storms and cyclones and earthquakes weeks beforehand, and will be invaluable to the world when the world gets to know of it.

This night I said as usual, 'Good evening, Professor. Have you had a nice day?' or words to that effect.

'Today I have been to see the King,' he said in his slow, muddled voice.

'What king?'

'Your king – King of England.'

His voice is husky, but has a little squeak in it. The King of England came out on the squeak.

'*My!*' (as Cynthia would say). A stir went round the *Pension* table. I distinctly heard the Hawkinses' ears prick. The little baby fern quivered. A tremble of excitement passed over the tails of the pheasants. And oh, how proud I felt that I sat next the man who had been talking to the King of England! I am sure if I had been a pheasant, I would have grown another tail on the spot, so that I could have done the occasion full justice and quivered adequately.

'You know the King, then?' I asked.

'The Archduke of Austria gif me letter imbroduction.'

'You know the Archduke of Austria?'

'He help me with my fern.'

With the most guileless simplicity he poured out slowly the names of half the crowned and coroneted heads in Europe.

Evidently they had not taken away his appetite. He sent for an enormous helping of roast beef to follow his pheasant as we talked.

Cynthia, Elfreda and Gertrude gazed at him with eyes that plainly said, 'Oh, man, how can you eat?'

But to him there was no reason why he should not have all the pheasant, roast beef, Yorkshire pudding and baked potatoes he could get. Life does not mean kings and arch-dukes and coronets to him. It has but two significations – a lot of food and a little fern. For he is a simple foreigner and a very great man.

So the winter wears on.

A wonderful winter it is. Full of new sensations, fresh glamour, shops, lovely, haunting, atmospheric effects, black trees, new friends, new customs, music – oh, above all! – music. As much Schumann, Chopin and Beethoven as one can hold. One week is marked by a symphony, another by a song. Through some days pulses the throb of the 'cello. Some are golden and im-mortalised by a woman's voice soaring above a great orchestra. Violins and violoncellos, and string quartets and trios, and orchestras, and tenors, and baritones, and sopranos, and contraltos, and organs in cathedrals and abbeys, and choirs in the chill morning and dim after-noon, and dense night, and the piano breathing Chopin and Beethoven and Mozart under the fingers of the world's greatest players – these are what my first winter in London is made of.

But why do I tell you of it, heartless creature that I am?

There are you all, thirsting for one little draught from this magic cup that I drink from day after day, week after week, month after month.

Dearests, that is the only cloud on my first winter: that I should have all this and you should stay at home twelve thousand miles away, and go to concerts in your great, beautiful, white town hall, and hear the biggest town hall organ in the world played without a single old stained window to help it, and go to the art gallery down there in the green domain at the harbour's edge, and look at our one Leighton, 'Wedded'[21], and one Vicat Cole, 'Arundel Castle'[22], and one marble Onslow Ford[23] – and no Turners, no Tintorettos, no Titians, no Raphaels, no Rubenses, no Vandykes, no Velasquez, not one single old master, and only half-a-dozen good modern ones. It is terrible to think of it.

To take the edge off your longing, I will tell you two facts. Yes, even I.

First, you would all go mad for a while over the great Bath Question. It makes all Australians mad. To come to London, the world's centre, and find big houses full of highly civilised people and no bathroom gives one an unpleasant shock. Yet there it is, this fact. People here can face life with one little shallow bath-pan kept in their own bedrooms.

I understand how the legend about Englishmen and the cold tub originated. It is literally a *tub* they patronise; they are not aquatic; they dislike cold water. It must be so; or London would not endure what seems to us a misery beyond words – the absence of bathrooms.

Of course, there are some, just a few.

Two weeks ago our landlord, who wants to get lots of Australians here, had a real genuine bath, and shower and water, set up in his third storey. Oh, the joy of it! And now Lizzie, the housemaid, is told off to discover who has had a bath and who has to pay sixpence for it.

The two jolly Australian students make great fun of this.

---

[21] Frederic, Lord Leighton's painting 'Wedded' was purchased by the Art Gallery of New South Wales in 1882.

[22] Vicat Cole's 'Arundel Castle at Sunset' was purchased by the Art Gallery of New South Wales in 1884.

[23] Edward Onslow Ford's sculpture 'Study of a Head' was purchased by the Art Gallery of New South Wales in 1897.

'Well, Lizzie, did you catch anyone today?' they ask her merrily.

That Austrian professor is a very honest man. Every morning he walks deliberately up to Lizzie and tells her seriously, 'I haf one bath.'

Emmie says it is an awful thing to have to pay somebody else sixpence because you keep yourself clean. She says she hesitates between the disgrace of having no baths to own up to, and the crime of having to pay sixpence for each confession.

And the other fact, what is it?

Is it a fact, I wonder?

It is that in all the great and sweet music I have heard this winter, in all the new pictures, and plays, and people, there is much to seek.

It is that the art world at present is striving for merely a technical perfection, rather than for magnificence, fire, pomp, grandeur, passion, insouciance, growth, freedom. For these are wanting, lacking everywhere in art, books, music, drama. All is hedged and clipped. The manners of the age surround its art. Everyone is trying to do something. The air is charged with students' pedantic notions. The masters spend their time teaching the students. They have no time to be free or to grow.

Or so it seems to your worldly-wise.

SYLVIA.

CHAPTER XIII

LONDON, *January* 190—.

DEAR EVERYONE,

Peter says to tell him particulars about some music. I never did before, 'cause – well, I had to hear a lot before I heard any.

He asks if I have heard a great player.

What is a Great Player, a Great Pianist?

Everyone in the world will give you a different description. Each to his own needs first, and, in proportion as these are satisfied, so is the music maker great.

To me, the great one is the one who takes me away from petty thoughts. The greatest is the one who absolutely prevents me from thinking at all. Bad art, but high joy. In Heaven one thinks not, neither does one know bad art from good.

Why not judge of him that way as well as any other, since music forever leads nowhere? It opens all gates, unlocks all doors, gives a wild, fleeting revelation of everything, then turns you out and leaves you there, alone in darkness, looking towards all things, unable to reach any.

Here he comes, the yellow-haired, the sleek-eyed man with the vague face that looks as if carven carefully out of a dream.

He seats himself, and his yellow head stands out against the black gown of a woman in the row behind the piano. His eye and nose are silhouetted too, the full drooped lid of the artist, the nose that is at once sensitive and generous. And the yellowy moustache and chin-tuft hiding a mouth that is compressed a little, and is graven about with fine pain – this, then, is the Great Player.

So we see him, looking at him for the first time – a vague, yellow face in yellow hair; gentle, but carrying somewhere between the narrowing lids a hint of tiger-fire.

He plays. Hush! hush! He plays softly to quieten the house of women. A chord is struck in warning, then a run floats across the hall, hushing all away.

What is he playing? What does it matter? Name it or not, it is *you* who give it its meaning. Well, then, since you demand, I will tell you he is playing *Études Symphoniques* – Schumann's.

The Great Player and Schumann; they chase the idea up and down, in and out of Érard,[24] and a faint voice from within whispers that he lacks in some subtle shade of fineness, making his transitions too marked for such a poet.

For such a poet! Ay, there's the rub. For the poet that he could be, is he quite poet enough?

And then he touches the piano with two 'Songs without Words', slowly, very, *very* slowly, lagging, dreaming.

Will Beethoven wake him?

---

[24] Sébastien Érard (1752–1831) was a renowned piano maker from Paris.

But that yellow vagueness is not for Beethoven. Music, breathing and thundering out the highest metaphysics, the essence of spiritual fervours, the message of a giant brain – these are not for that face carved out of a dream.

Give him Schubert-Liszt, give him Chopin, and the king comes into his own.

He takes the piano into his hand like a brush, and paints on the flexible molten brain of his audience a storm, a torture – 'Der Erl König'.[25] He dashes it in with a passionless force till the house flees with him in the wild flight – but leaving its body here behind it in St James's Hall, with the rain beating on the roof – yes, always leaving its body here behind it. He takes the soul, but leaves the body to consciousness.

And then Chopin – a ballade, two preludes, etudes, a mazurka, a polonaise. They float, they float; they caress the soul.

The yellow hair gets in its work, and the tiger-fire flashes with the strange, indifferent passion of a poet. His runs are like streaks of silver flung across the spirit.

Runs! Oh, hideous word! The crudeness and clumsiness of the English language can show no uglier example than that word 'Runs'. *Runs!* – for that tongue of flame leaping across the piano! RUNS! – for that dash of spray in the sunlight! RUNS! – for that long, thin streak of lightning that flashes across the heart, firing the inner eye with silver, stealing the breath, leaving one dizzy, dazed, and thrilled.

In the Great Player's hands a run is like an 'Oh!' in some moment of sudden spiritual exaltation.

---

[25] Franz Schubert's 'Der Erlkönig'(1815) was a musical rendition of Goethe's 1782 poem of the same name.

Just as the poet cries 'Oh God!' 'Oh, my love!' the Player sends up these silver cries. It is hours since I heard him, but I see the colour of his runs still. Silver – always silver.

Until I heard him play, I never heard the message of a cascade of notes. I saw it as an ornament, and turned aside a little. With the unnecessary cruelty of the ignorant I called it vulgar, and drew away, admiring, but never knowing, never taking it to myself.

Till he played those preludes. Then I was punished; and all my days I'll go the softlier, sadlier for my crime's sake.

Jean said, 'I don't like the way he lifts his hands; it's so *affected*.'

But I thought of the runs, and I said to myself, 'For this vague man with the mouth of pain, there is some hidden meaning – even to those hands thrown back, held back, posed back, theatrically.'

And I found the meaning after a time. His pose of hand is the expression of his soul, his condition of emotion. Sometimes his hand flies up and remains dead still, the fingers bent. It stays like that for a full moment. Jean says 'affectation'. It seems a long, long time before it comes down again. If you don't know what it means you grow a little uneasy, overstrained; but if you understand, if you watch his eyes, his lips, listen to his music and get into his region, you will find he is venting himself in those raised hands, just as you bite your lip in sudden danger, just as you open your eye in great surprise, just as you lift your hands at some dread message. Those taut, raised hands are the expression of his mood.

But *great* – is this Great Player *great*?

Not to a craving, exacting imagination, that demands fire and dew together; that cries for the heavens to be opened and solid earth to be swept from beneath its feet. He plays forever in a dream. He translates Chopin inimitably, with perfect grace, with despair, with a lovely charm and a veiled passion; but the homely flower-feeling, the domestic, pure love in Mendelssohn's music, was blurred with a sentimentality that had no place there. He played those two 'Songs without Words' with a drawn-out tenderness that grew thin from very slowness. And in a Beethoven sonata (Op. iii) the struggle between the Great Player and the greatest musical genius of all time was to the strong. Beethoven conquered; the player was left behind. He has neither the grandeur of style nor mind for this immortal.

Give him the songs he knows to sing, and he is superb.

They say he plays to women. Well, but what then! So do all artists; everyone who plays to an audience – the poet, the actor, the artist, the writer, the pianist, the singer – it's to women he is appealing, or to the woman in a man.

Now I appeal to the woman in you, Pete. Isn't this true? Your loving

SILVER.

CHAPTER XIV

LONDON, *February* 190—.

DEAR EVERYBODY,

Have you ever heard of something called 'The London Hump'? I am afraid poor Emmie has it.

It is a terrible thing to watch, this struggle of a girl with London. Here is Emmie with her voice, a glorious contralto, her brains, her ambitions, her years of study, fighting a bitter fight that takes all the colour out of her life and the light out of her eyes. While she was merely studying she was the happiest creature alive. But as soon as the battle with the agents began, and she has to stand up before the great test – will London have her or have none of her? – she becomes the most nervous, miserable girl, with a perpetual load of disappointment to carry and a sick fear. The dread of facing her own land again, where everyone knows everyone, and where those who come to London are being watched with hungry scrutiny over all those thousands of miles – that is what unnerves her so. Australia expects so much from her own.

Poor Emmie! I see her long form stretched on my bed at this very moment. She came in here after lunch, burst into tears, and cried bitterly in my arms. Then I put a wet handkerchief on her head, covered her up with my 'possum-skin rug, and made her lie quiet for a while.

In this life in a boarding house one lives to oneself. The hands do nothing for anyone else. The feet run no loving errands. The day is mapped out with duties and pleasures, all centred around oneself.

And after a time the hands ache to do little things for someone else. The arms want someone to go round. It would be a pleasure to *have* to do some little tasks for someone else dear.

It is human nature asserting itself. It creeps up, up, through the stratum of boarding house life, till it pierces its way through, and cannot be gainsaid. Men and women alike want someone for whom to do something.

And then Emmie comes to me crying, and I hold her in my arms and hug her tight, and the blessedness of having someone warm and close to comfort and console strikes a note that is almost gladness.

Dear Emmie! Her long black hair lies all over my pillow. Her violet eyes are shut, but I can see them as I write – candid, roguish eyes that look at you with a boy's glance. I love her laugh, a sudden cascade of low notes that gush up deliciously. One of the nicest things I know is to make Emmie laugh.

Poor Emmie! Some days she dashes about her room, and in and out of mine, exclaiming ludicrously, 'Ambition is a curse!' Or, 'Blessed is the girl who is born dumb!' Or, 'Happy is the woman who is born without ambition!'

Now it has come to this. She does not care if she fails. She does not care if she succeeds. She cares for nothing. She does not want to go home. She does not want to stay here. For the moment she is broken down and has lost her hold on life. She feels the cold. It oppresses her. She coughs, and her voice gets thick, and she grows more and more melancholy.

Other Australian girls who are getting on well in London come to tea with us and tell us their 'views'. One, a brilliant popular singer, says that when she comes home alone to her flat at night after a success before the public she tosses her cloak savagely on to her couch and says to herself, 'This is a dog's life.'

And here is Emmie, a girl made to be happy, crying her eyes out for 'a dog's life'. How little of this do the girls in Australia know!

The endless succession of rebuffs, disappointments, chilling receptions, the continual need to fight – these are all hidden from them. Would they venture here so gaily, so fearlessly, if they understood?

And now I want to explain to you a very queer thing about London.

When this queer thing comes home to you, you have learned the largeness of this city.

At first we Australians are all surprised to find London so small. That is because our eyes are accustomed to great distances, and because we judge by what we see. We think we are looking at all London. Months and months after, we begin to realise that it is impossible ever to look at London.

Only in fragments can this great city be taken into the eye. We can but see one piece at a time. Our first impression is that all is so much smaller than we expected. But by-and-by comes the hour when we go out to do battle with London. Then comes home to us its immensity.

We start off, hopeful, eager, one day when there is no fog. As we leave our house our thoughts are keen and edged. We carry a strong purpose in our brain. We know what we want to do. We believe we can do it. We know what we want to get. We believe we shall get it. We leave the neighbourhood of houses. We begin to get into the city. An infinity of buildings meets us. Streams of people pass. One face after another enters into our consciousness.

And every building, every face, steals something from us.

They are not glad faces. They are cold and reserved. They are stamped with marks of the battle for life.

Oh, the pain and the strain in these faces in the street! And, oh, the coldness, the aloofness!

A street in Sydney rises and flashes across the memory. We see around us warm mixed-grey eyes, deep set and full of expression. We see men with tanned skins. That note of red in their faces carries cheer with it. London faces are so white and fixed. We see those loose tweed clothes and soft hats and shirts. We find relief in the diversity of their clothing. Some wear top hats, some wear sailor-straws, some are in white, some in brown, some in grey. And the women have mobile, languid faces, and veils floating from their shady hats, and laughing mouths. No one is stiff or starched. Everyone is intensely alive. And the glance of them is warm with frank friendship and *camaraderie*. They all look at each other as if they all exist. And for strangers the glance is kinder even than for each other.

And as we walk among them, with hope in our hearts, they deepen the hope, they strengthen the conviction, they quicken the pulse, they lighten the heart.

Here, how different! Every street robs us of our faith in ourselves.

Bit by bit our confidence crumbles and drops away from us. Oh, the stony hardness of the buildings, the great massing together of determined and resistant forces, the innumerable uninterested eyes, the tight-closed lips, the misery of the miserable, the indifference of the affluent, the proud mask of the happy!

We are in business quarters. These people are all about their business. The effort to live imprisons them. Whether *you* live or not matters nothing. You begin presently to believe it matters nothing.

And, above all, there is something about the buildings that tells you what a mere atom you are. Office upon office looks down on you. You gaze upwards from storey to storey. To think of making an impression on them! At every higher flight you lose so much of your courage.

They steal from you all your need for your battle. They dissipate your will. They weaken your intention. They convince you of your unimportance.

You arrive at your destination in wonder at your coming. Why are you here? What do you seek? Work? A chance? A hearing? Why should you expect any of these? Who are you? No one. What are you worth? Nothing. Who wants you? Nobody.

And your work, what does it matter?

Oh, nothing, nothing, nothing does it matter.

And so, in that one walk, between the time of closing your house door behind you and arriving at the place of business where you meant to present yourself and seek for work, you have lost all that is likely to help you in the search. Your belief in yourself has flown. The faces in the streets, the miles and miles of buildings, the great, cruel indifference of the massed city, have struck cold to your heart. Life and light and hope have left you. Courage and vitality have been deliberately stolen from you ever since you left your house.

And the object of your journey has turned paltry and dim. You are so small, so unimportant, beside *all this*. You have shrivelled from a great, glowing, hopeful ego to a worm that believes its only use is to crawl out of other people's way.

When you know you are only a worm you are not surprised to find that everyone else recognises the fact also. It seems right and just that your wormhood should find its full recognition here – among other worms.

And so you turn back, perhaps, unable to crawl up the steps of an office, and pretend that you can do something. All the way back home you go again.

It is not that you are afraid to attempt. It is that you have lost all sense of values. Nothing seems worth attempting.

That is the cruellest moment the hopeful Australian encounters here. The change from the conditions of his own land is so stupendous that he feels this moment far more bitterly than any Englishman. He is used to the kind glances of his own country, where offices never frown, but stand with their doors open wide, wearing a simple, friendly, accessible air that is nowhere to be found in London.

'As long as I never go out,' says Emmie, 'I believe I shall get on.'

But to stay in the house and believe in yourself is not the way to get on. We must go out and face the massed buildings, those cruel, implacable thieves that steal our vitality, and confront the innumerable faces whose expressions depress us. We must learn to keep hope warm in our hearts even among these freezing conditions.

That's where the battle comes in. Not to be crushed, not to have the purpose dissipated, is a hard struggle for an Australian in London. At home, the blue of the sky, the dazzling gold of the sunlight, the warmth and friendliness of the faces around, are all massed on the side of the fighter. In losing them here one loses so much of one's defence.

I began this letter yesterday, and take it up today to tell you we are going to move.

It is not my secret, so I cannot tell you more than this – it will be better for Emmie to go away. There is a man here, and he is a foreigner, and Emmie doesn't want to break anyone's heart.

Your loving

SYLVIA.

CHAPTER XV

LONDON, *March* 190—.

MY DEARESTS,

I know how you think of me now. I can see the picture you have of me. You are always saying to yourselves, 'However will she stand it?' You imagine me trying day and night to get warm. You see a monster steadily coming down on me, a big, fierce, implacable monster. It crushes me slowly, until I cry with pain and fright, and wish I were home again, and grow sick with pining for my sunny skies and warm air. You call the monster by the name of London Winter.

I came here with that monster haunting me. Even in the hot summer, 'Wait till the winter,' I kept saying. 'Then the terror of London will come home to you.' I used to ask everyone questions.

'Is the cold so very frightful?'

'Can you go about in the house without a jacket over your blouse?'

'Can you possibly sit in a room without a fire?'

'Could you *possibly* ride outside on a 'bus?'

'Could you get warm in bed if you had enough blankets?'

'Would the water be always frozen in your jug?'

'Didn't the cold paralyse everyone and make them unable to work?'

'Wasn't it frightful? Wasn't it awful? Wasn't it too terrible?'

If London Winter were what we imagined it, there would be nobody alive in London. In our thoughts it was something so monstrous, so implacable, fierce, cruel, persistent, that – now I come to think of it in the midst of it – I can see how impossible it would be for anyone to survive it.

I wonder why we never said to ourselves, 'Think of the millions who *live* in London.'

Coming away, everyone said, 'How will you stand the winter?' And every time they said it, a little sick fear used to thrill down my backbone. What a heroine I was! I used to boldly take that thrill and choke it, and say to myself, with a stern resolve, 'If I have to, I'll *die*.'

'Oh, the winter, the winter,' cried everyone overseas. Most of those who had been to London left before the winter. Those who had stayed through it were unable to describe the terrors of it.

'You will be like little Georgie,' said Ethel Smith. 'His sister came down to breakfast one morning and said the water in her jug was frozen. Was the water frozen in your jug, Georgie?' she asked.

'I never looked to see,' said Georgie.

With such cheerful anecdotes they prepared me for what I had to face.

At last I completed my fancy picture of London Winter. Gathering together all they told me, and filling gaps with my own imagination, I produced a winter that would take a gold medal at any season's exhibition.

Winter! Ugh! The sun is never seen. We rise in the pitch dark, break the ice in the jug, dress ourselves in flannels, and vests, and over-vests, and blouses and jackets, and layer after layer of woollen petticoats. We breakfast by gaslight, we lunch by gaslight, we dine by gaslight. The middle of the day it is just light enough to grope our way through the streets. Every day there is a fog. We dare not go out. Traffic is continually suspended. People are forever getting lost and being brought home by policemen. Enormous fires can do nothing to make the rooms warmer. It is absolutely impossible to get warm, even in the fire. At three o'clock, pitch darkness closes down on the city again. Snow falls, and streets turn white, and shivering crossing-sweepers clean the steps. On and on, week after week, month after month, this terrible winter holds you in its grasp. You never once see the sun. The city is shrouded in perpetual dark grey mist. You never once feel warm. You are sad, gloomy, despairing. You yearn and pine for the spring. That is London Winter as I believed it was going to be.

And the real thing, how is it?

I am almost afraid to tell you. Humbly, deprecatingly, I lop off the heads of your pet superstitions, upset colonial traditions, and present you with London Winter as it showed itself to me.

To my Australian eyes London Winter is crowded with beauty. It is so strange, so unreal, that I can scarce believe I am part of it. If I stay indoors for some days I am pierced afresh with keen surprise when I go out again. One cannot, all suddenly, grow used to the new heavens or the new earth. Particularly to the new heavens, stranger even than the strange, blank new earth.

Up there wonderful things happen. When I go walking I cannot take my eyes from the sky and the beautiful winter sun. No sun in London? Why, I have come to know more suns this winter in London than in a lifetime in sunny Australia.

For in Australia the sun is part of life, as the air is, and the earth. It is there to shine and burn, not to be seen. It is too bright to be looked at. Long, fierce rays shoot out all round it, blinding the eye. Even in winter it will not allow you to stare. It sets a dazzling network of golden rays around it, and fires its gold far, far out into the sky.

But the London sun in winter hovers aloft gently, like a blood-red, rayless moon. You can look, and look, and look. There are no beams to blind you. Nurse-girls wheel babies in perambulators over you. Curious men and women stop to see what you are standing still to look at, then pass on in vexation without finding it. They wanted a balloon or house on fire, something that started on earth and would be worth looking at. That red sun is nothing to them. They have had it all their lives, never looked at it yet, and are not going to begin now. But the red sun stays on, indifferent. The red sun is above all that.

As I write, pictures rise and flash across me. Midday, Trafalgar Square. The sky one great sheet of softest grey, like a scarf of chiffon, grey, deep, yet unsubstantial somehow. There are no clouds. The grey scarf floats from end to end of the sky. In the very middle of the grey is the sun, high up, above Nelson's Monument. Nelson seems reaching up towards it.

Far, far away it looks. A red ball, a deep, glowless, rayless, rose-red. And as I watch, it quietly sinks back, back, into the great billow, till only a wide, dull flush shows that it is still somewhere behind the veil.

A feeling of midnight, of a setting autumn moon, steals over me. I am in London in the middle of the day. But that sky and sun have nothing to do with midday and the clamour of a great city. Near is the playing fountain, with strange, dull lights on it. And there the proud, reserved-looking National Gallery, with its hidden treasures. And across the square, the long pillar, rearing up and up, with the sailor figure at the top silhouetted brownly against the wide, faint flush. And it is London and the middle of the day.

Oh, Spirit of the Beautiful, ever hovering near, how strangely you manifest yourself! Sometimes you come to us on tender memories, you steal out of a Past, and transfigure plain places because our youth was weaved into them. Sometimes you sweep, in sublime positivism, across all our dreams and ideals, crush them, and rear yourself on their graves, crying, '*I* am Beauty. Here is no doubt.' And sometimes, and this is your sweetest, keenest revelation, you flash out of contrasts, as a spark leaps from stones brought suddenly together.

So it is that red, moon-like sun sinking back into the thick, grey sky, one workaday noon in the loudest, busiest city in the world, speaks to me of beauty so insistently that I can only stand and stare, unable to move on for a long time.

Another picture: again all sky and sun.

A long, shadowy street in Bloomsbury. On either side are high, brown houses. In the valley between hovers all day a pale, ethereal mist, sometimes full of dim violets and blues, sometimes a heavy, rose-flushed yellow. I stand at the beginning of the street. Away at the far end hovers a burning orange lantern. It seems to belong to nothing, to have no grasp on the firmament, no close setting of sky to keep it in its place, no sunbeams, no rays shooting out of it. It is the sun, but I can scarcely believe it. Oh, lonely, rayless, isolated sun, burning, companionless, in the grey sky, you fill me with joy! I am glad I am a stranger, because I bring you fresh, young adoration, deepening slowly into tender, intimate knowledge.

It is the absence of rays that makes this London sun so lonely and isolated. You can see the curving edge of it. You can see a long way round the curve. And you can almost see through it. Is it indeed the sun? Sometimes I refuse to believe it. I am convinced it is only a lantern – a red Chinese lantern. To me a sun means something sparkling, glittering, shooting diamonds and rubies all day long. Jewels and metals are not to be found in this new sun. It is not there to warm or dazzle. Perhaps, then, it is there just to be loved, so I love it, and watch it like a mother.

The afternoons are filled with ever-increasing happiness. Something I wanted all my life is here. It creeps into me from the violet-misted streets, from the rose and yellow fogs, the orange suns, the grey chiffon skies, the black, delicate trees.

I hear people sighing for the winter to be over, but I am hoarding up every minute of it, hating it to pass.

Every afternoon, away in far Australia, there comes over us all a half-past-two-in-the-afternoon feeling, an intolerable *ennui*, a sense of emptiness and discontent, a longing for something large and full that cannot be exhausted. Men, and women, and boys, and girls, all know the feeling. The bright blue sky, blazing away overhead, the endless golden sunlight, the vivid rivers and creeks, become monotonous. Something is wanting. Even the busiest man and woman is overcome with this *ennui* at times. Half past two in the afternoon is the most fatal hour, because then one becomes conscious that there is nothing to do but to repeat the morning.

It is our remoteness that pains us. We are so far, far off. Our veins run warm with English blood, and London calls, calls, and we are there, a whole world away. That is the meaning of the half-past-two-in-the-afternoon feeling. It is a sudden sense of our great distance from the full intellectual life of the Old World, from music and art.

I had it often. I lost it when I came to London. At half past two in the afternoon now there rolls over one a great, gorgeous wave of intense happiness. All the things I can see flash over me. In vivid succession there rush through the brain Turner's watercolours downstairs under the National Gallery, records of his inspired flights in Italy, in Germany, in Switzerland, with that lovely moist dimness hovering about them; the strange sky and sun outside; the strange parks full of black trees; the shops, unending; the people, never to be wearied of; big music, that never comes to an end, that does not come to us for a brief visit then fly away and leave us thirstier than ever after that one short draught; sweet, strange, atmospheric effects; a winter that lasts nearly long enough; people with the charm and glamour of other lands clinging to them.

Oh, London, London! How did I ever live without you? I no longer go about asking in an awestricken voice, 'Is this *the* Soho?' 'Is that *the* Regent Street?' 'Is this *the* Piccadilly?' I no longer say to myself, '*You're in London.*'

I accept it at last, and surrender to the spell of the City of Mists.

It never seems to me crowded, and dense, and dark. There are great spaces in my brain, and yellow sunlight. When I dream at nights the setting of my dreams is Australia. So when I wake in the morning I have the consciousness of a wide, free country all about me. I carry Australia around with me, and its paddocks and plains open out in the heart of London, and make room in the densest places. Sometimes when I look out, first thing in the morning, before I see the brown houses opposite, I see Sydney Harbour lying like violet glass under a fleckless summer sky, and the ferry boats crossing and re-crossing, taking people to work in the city at the harbour's edge.

One more picture, a little one.

St James's Park one February afternoon; a pale grey sky, nearly white; a pale, cold, gold sun; a broad, green grass slope planted with bare black trees fretted with indescribable loveliness against the white sky and pale gold sun.

The white sky reaches right to the ground. It ends there in a white, feathery, floating mist, veiling the far-off trees and shrubs and people.

Down under the sun a tone of golden mauve makes itself felt rather than seen.

And all this delicate, ethereal white and mauve and gold in the very heart of London – London, the City of the Great Smoke, as we always call it over there.

In November the sky stands still. All through November, December, January and February it remains motionless. I believe someone in authority hangs a curtain over the clouds to keep them warm till the winter is gone.

But in March, in March, the sky, like the earth, wakes up. It begins to move again. The chiffon veil drops off. Clouds begin to roll over the fields up there. Such clouds!

They look as if they had rolled through paradise before they got into the Earth's sky. They have bathed themselves in opal rivers and rose lakes. Over the sky they roll and roll, all March through.

And the million windows of the million houses blaze and glow as if they, too, had nothing to do with Earth.

Next year, perhaps, I shall not notice them. But the first time of seeing a great grey sky break up, and let its clouds out after months and months of dead grey stillness, is as full of wonder as any flower or tree change.

As for the *cold* – the terrible, dreaded monster – well, I scarcely noticed it. There was so much else to think of.

Only, to satisfy your curiosity about purely mundane things – the water in my jug never, never froze, and I wore silk blouses in the house *without* a jacket in the very depths of winter.

I do not say I have never been cold. Some days I have been conscious of a hard, oppressive something in the atmosphere that made me speak slowly, and hurt my hands. But I can honestly say the winter cold on our Blue Mountains seemed far, far sharper, fiercer, louder, and more aggressive, than London Winter.

This is not the picture of London Winter you are expecting. I quite realise how keen your disappointment will be. I *could* tell you, too, that a fog turns the city houses to fairy palaces lit with fairy lanterns that shine softly through the fairy yellow atmosphere, but I dare not. You might cable for me to come home. You know so well all the horrors and terrors of fog that I could never *convince* you of my sanity if I attempted to gild 'pea-soup'.

¹ No, I'll leave you that. You can hug its horridness to your breasts and pity me all you like. I really am almost afraid to tell even myself what I found in my first fog.

Wait, wait, wait. Don't believe what anyone tells you, 'cept me. Wait till you come and see for yourselves.

Your sun-struck

SILVER.

CHAPTER XVI

March-end 190—.

MY DEAR PEOPLE,

Emmie and I have gone up in the world. We no longer live in a boarding house. We have raised our heads into apartments, two storeys up.

There are three grades of homelessness in London – boarding house, apartments, flat.

If you live in boarding houses you cannot be known. If you live in apartments you can go and see your friends. If you have a flat your friends can come and see you.

That, my dear, rustic chicks, is the correct English attitude to these three common conditions of alien life in London.

Well, we have moved, as I said. And now we are no longer Emmie Jones and Sylvia Leighton. We have left all that behind us.

We are something rather less complicated and more easy to describe. We are the Drawing Rooms.

Underneath us live some people called the Dining Rooms. Above us dwell folk yclept[26] Third Floors. Above

---

[26] An archaic word meaning called or named.

them again exist some stray solitaries in bed-sitting rooms. And these are all the inhabitants in our new location, except the two landladies and the three maids.

It was hard to say goodbye to the foreign countries and the elm, but there are foreigners all around, and there are trees here too. They do not tap against the window frame, but I can see right into them and through them from all parts of my bedroom. As I sit at the piano I can look away through a black fretwork of bare planes to the sunset. And at twilight I can watch from my armchair the square and the street around it grow bluer and bluer, and the street lamps glow out of the blue in vivid orange discs. We never see orange like that in Australia.

And it's nearly spring, March-end, and there are pale green pearls at the end of all the big and little black twigs and branches.

Alice, the fair, fat, untidy housemaid that waits upon us here, brings a pure Cockney element into our lives that fills us with joy – not unmixed with pain – to continue that sentence in the way it should go.

'There's them Dinin' Rooms ringin' away agen,' says Alice as she sets our breakfast table.

'I suppose Dining Rooms want breakfast as well as Drawing Rooms.'

'Oh, it isn't their wantin' their breakfasses. It's their demandin' wiay of talkin' to you *I* mind.'

Alice is a high-spirited creature, like all English servants. The submissive nature which is supposed to be characteristic of English women has not entered into the English servant class. Australian servants 'give cheek'. English servants pour forth insults. Australian servants won't get up early and will stay out late. English servants have frequently to be put out of the house by a police-man. They summon their mistresses, they refuse to do anything outside their own line, they will not be 'generals'. They are greedy and grasping because their wages are so low, and because they sodden themselves with constant beer and stout.

To the Australian housewife there is one dear, longed-for luxury, one dream she indulges vainly – the possession of an English servant. She believes there is no handmaid on earth equal to an English servant. She fills herself with fancies of one cleaning her doorsteps at half past four in the morning, cooking to perfection, and turning her house into a shining paradise. Well, far be it from me to take away any of the rare dreams of a good and unimagi-native housewife. I will maintain a discreet silence. And when I come home I won't bring an English maid with me.

Last week I fell a victim to influenza. It attacked me sud-denly. I had been out to the theatre and came home with a frightful head. I could scarcely endure to undress myself. I wanted to fall like a log on my bed and never move again. However, I did take off my clothes, and as a big wastepaper basket stood near my bed I dropped some of my garments in there and crept to bed to a night of agony.

Next morning I was very ill and remained in bed for a week.

The following day Alice came in with a cup of tea. Having given it to me, she sat down on the edge of an arm-chair in front of the fire and gazed dreamily into the coals. This is her favourite method of getting on with her work.

Presently she put forth one foot and a fat leg, and looked at them critically.

'Don't look bad, do it?' said she.

I raised my head a little to look. I saw a fat leg bursting out of a rather pretty black stocking embroidered in mauve. It looked familiar.

'What is it?' I asked.

'Yourn stockin's,' she replied. 'I washed 'em out last night. They fit me grand.'

Light broke on me.

'Did you take them out of the basket?' I cried.

'Yes. And Kyte 'as the woollens. We divided. She washed 'em out last night and 'as 'em on now.'

I was first angry, then annoyed. Then the humour of the situation burst on me as I looked at Alice's fat calf bursting out of my best evening stockings, and I could do nothing but laugh weakly, especially when I reflected that Alice gave the other garments to Kyte because she could not possibly get into them herself.

That was rather quick practice, was it not?

Now I hope I speak without prejudice, but am fearful that I do not, when I say that with all the familiarity and 'casualness' of the Australian domestic she would never come by her mistress's clothes in that sharp way. If she steals she steals; and she rarely steals. But then her wages are sixteen shillings a week. Alice earns sixteen pounds a year.

Her brain is a remarkable study. I sometimes take it out and dissect it. I find it mixed inextricably with eggs and bacon, and stairs, and the lighting of fires, and beer, and left-off dresses, and bells and trays, and little teapots. It is unmistakably an apartment brain. There are even 'apartments to let' in it.

Every day at lunch she has a bottle of beer. And every night, before she goes to bed, she has another. Fourteen bottles of beer a week. Sixty bottles of beer a month. Seven hundred and thirty bottles of beer a year. She has been at service since she was fourteen. She has imbibed over six thousand bottles of beer. Think of it!

Is it any wonder that apartments continue to be let inside her brain? If a thought entered to take lodgings it would at once be swamped.

All day long this strange girl pants up and down stairs. All the 'guests' dine in their own rooms, and Alice spends her days carrying up meals and clearing them away again. She has a long way to go. The kitchen is down in the basement, and those six thousand bottles of beer on the brain never permit her to exercise her ingenuity and plan how to spare herself. She has a little tray ready for Top Floors' lunch. She looks at it a second. She sees two little covered dishes, a loaf of bread, butter, cheese, glasses, plates, knives. She picks it up and carries it off. Arrived at the top floor, she finds she has forgotten the forks. Down she goes, not grumbling, but murmuring little invectives at herself. On her way down the Dining-Room bell rings. She passes it and trudges on after her forks. She finds them, pants upstairs again. On her way up she stops at the Dining Rooms. 'Did yourn want anything?' Yes, she has forgotten their cheese. They want it at once. Alice sighs, goes out, and pants on up to the top of the house, where the Top Floors have discovered by this time that she has forgotten their cruet. 'Well, what do you think of that for a 'ead?' says Alice. 'I won't never spare my legses.' Off she goes again, away down, down, down to the very basement. The drawing room bell is ringing; but she lets it ring. She collects the cheese for the Dining Rooms, and the cruet for the Top Floors, and starts off once more on that terrible journey upstairs. The Drawing-Room bell is now ringing angrily, so she opens the door as she passes to see what is wanted. They want their dishes taken away and some jam brought up. Luckily for her peace of mind she does not see that she could have saved this if she had gone in here last journey. I leave it to your mathematical abilities to discover how many stairs she *might* have spared herself this one lunchtime if she had answered her bells in different order.

I know that a head full of beer and bells ringing could not be conducive to elegance of speech, but I never cease to wonder at the strange twists Alice gives words.

She must have heard the word 'artichokes' hundreds of times in this house, but she has never come to see that it is not '*chartieoak*'.

If the landladies go out and leave her to see any possible callers after a vacant room they instruct her in the terms and usual technicalities, and Alice invariably inquires, 'Is that *conclusive*?' 'Yes, these terms are inclusive,' invariably replies Miss Greene. But Alice never notices.

Before we met her, Alice was an utterly unknown quantity to us. At home a servant who drinks beer gets herself into serious trouble. Here the mistress not only overlooks, she *provides*. It is she herself who gives out the beer from her own cupboards. It was a long time before we could approve of that. We dubbed it a terrible custom. We included it among the strange old stubborn English customs we almost felt strong enough to reform.

Emmie still has the London Hump. She brought it along with her from the *Pension* to the apartments. It rides on her back like an Old Man of the Sea.

'I want to go home' is the burden of her cry.

She comes into my room late at night sometimes, and sits on the edge of my bed in her crimson wrapper, and she keeps me out of my beauty sleep while she asks if I remember how the Hawkesbury used to wind and shine in the moonlight at Easter. She meanders on about a boat she wants to be out in. And how she wants to wear a white frock again, and have her lap full of scarlet waratahs, and be rowing down the river towards Milson's Island, where there will be a billy to boil and a camp tea in the moonlight.

One night she reads me a little poem from a magazine:

> I want to go home
> To the dull old town,
> With the shaded streets,
> And the open square,
> And the hill,
> And the flats,
> And the house I love,
> And the paths I know.
> I want to go home.
>
> If I can't go back
> To the happy days,
> Yet I can live
> Where their shadows lie,
> Under the trees
> And over the grass.
> I want to be there,
> Where the joy was once;
> Oh, I want to go home,
> I want to go home.[27]

---

[27] A poem by Paul Kester (1870–1933), 'Home', published in the *Idler* in 1901–02. Kester was an American playwright and novelist.

She throws herself across my feet and buries her head in my quilt.

'Why do we come here?' says her stifled voice. 'They don't want *us*. If we can push our way into a little slit they allow us to stay there perhaps, but not because they *want* us, only because we pushed. I'm sick of pushing. I'm sick of trying. I'm sick of agents. I think the musical profession is the most contemptible in the whole world. A woman's success depends on how well she dresses and how bad she looks. I won't dress well. I won't look bad.'

'Rubbish!' crossly from under the bedclothes.

'Over in Australia are hundreds of girls with voices pining away because they cannot get to London. To get to London is all that is needed to make them famous. That is the common belief in Australia.'

'They know absolutely nothing of what really happens here.'

'I'll be the bitter example. I'll go home and say, "I failed. Couldn't get on. Nobody wanted me. It wasn't the climate in my case. It was pure failure. I didn't dress well, and I didn't look bad."'

'Em!'

'I'll be the first, the very first, to fail. Everyone else who ever came back without a career was driven away by the climate.'

'*Make* them want you. Your voice is better than anyone's.'

'Mr Jones today: "Why did you come here? Wasn't Australia big enough for you?" "Geographically it was," I replied.'

'Impertinence!'

'Not at all. He was quite right. Australia should have been big enough for me. I'm an Australian.'

She is a victim to colds, too. One follows another. Then she has influenza. Then a second attack of the same horrid illness. Her voice goes away altogether. She gets into the depths of misery, and I think seriously of inducing her to go back to Sydney to save her reason.

But with it all there is just one little redeeming ray of light – her sense of humour. Ah, pitiable indeed must be the struggle of a girl alien who has not that ineffable gold streak to gild her misery. Emmie often rises from her 'howls' and goes and looks at herself in the glass. A woman who can do that will never die of despair.

Sometimes a pang of envy seizes me. I thought I loved my country as passionately as anyone could love her. But I am not breaking my heart to go back. Is Emmie a better patriot than I? Is she truer and more faithful? I love every place I come to. The whole world fills me with rapture. I never realised its existence till I came to London. It was just the world on the map. Nothing was *real* but Australia.

I can see again that soft, late summer night, our boat stealing away from the harbour at Fremantle out into the darkness, the red lights of the coast fading, fading, Australia receding, my eyes brimming, my heart crying, 'Australia, Australia, I'll never love anyone but you.'

And now it is London I am in love with. If I had to leave London my eyes would fill with tears again and my heart would ache bitterly.

But no. I insist that this is not faithlessness. It is a deeper demonstration of my fidelity. I am faithful to the whole world, not to one little bit of her.

You must not think we do nothing but console and weep. I practise concertos and sonatas. Emmie goes on 'trying her luck', endeavouring to get her first hearing from a London audience. And we laugh lots. And talk – endlessly. And some of the people from the *Pension* come to see us sometimes, and we go out to supper and dinner at friends' houses occasionally. And we take long, long walks in the twilight, or the moonlight, about London.

Arm-in-arm we wander about. Nobody knows us. We know nobody. Emmie does a frightful calculation to show how many hours and days, for how many weeks you can go out in London without meeting anyone you know. Many a night, after a concert, we walk along the Embankment under the spindly trees, and Emmie sings 'Out on the Rocks' in a low, murmuring voice for my ear alone, and we hang over the stone wall and talk about Sydney and the gum trees, and look away into the mist on the Thames, with long chains of red lamplights gleaming along the far banks. We harrow ourselves a little, but we are immensely happy, even though Emmie is so miserable.

To walk arm-in-arm with a friend, to pace along under the night skies, to have a low, rich voice singing some old familiar song to you, to have London closing round you, this is ideal happiness. There is no better way of walking with a friend, of hearing music, or of knowing London, if you have come from Australia first.

In all our wanderings no one ever addresses us. The bold, bad men that are supposed to make walking at night impossible for respectable females never come across our path.

Miss Greene and Miss Lowe, our landladies, would not venture out together at night for any sum of money that no one is going to offer them. Miss Greene is fifty, Miss Lowe is forty. They have never been out of England. They nourish a dreadful opinion of their countrymen. They are sensational old ladies; they never go out without their cab horse slipping down or nearly running away with them, without a dog chasing them, or a motor car just escaping them. In fact, they seem to have been pursued by every animal save man.

One day a dreadful thing happens. Miss Greene comes up to our sitting room, enters, shuts the door, seats herself on the sofa, and says, in an excited whisper, 'Miss Leighton, there is a terrible thing going on here. Miss Leighton, I have been through so much and I cannot stand it.' Then she suddenly sparks up, for she is a spirited old lady underneath, with a droll sense of humour. 'I want to tell you, Miss Leighton and Miss Jones, not to take any notice of a tall man with white hair in blue clothes you may see downstairs. He is a bailiff.'

She comes near to crying again, but pluckily chokes away the tears. Just then another knock comes to the door, and Miss Lowe enters.

'Oh, Miss Leighton, isn't it terrible? Is Miss Greene telling you?'

Miss Lowe is a tall, very plump young woman, with light red hair, and a highly developed bust. She is just bordering on old maidenhood, and is remarkable for her devotion to old Miss Greene, who is also remarkable for her devotion to young Miss Lowe. That two such characters existed out of Dickens was something we never suspected.

'What is he doing, Harriet, darling?'

'Sitting on the chair in our sitting room, dearest.'

They look at each other in silence and then at us, and we all stare blankly, until Emmie inquires, half fearfully, 'Where did he come from?'

'It is a long story, Miss Jones,' says Miss Greene.

As she says that, I feel a little less sorry for her. Something in the tone of her voice tells me she finds a gleam of pleasure in having a long story to tell. It is a harrowing story, but the relish in her voice deepens as she goes on, aided, and interrupted, and contradicted, and confirmed by Miss Lowe.

'We took this house three months ago, Miss Leighton.'

'We took it, on the understanding that it was full, Miss Leighton. The woman showed us over, and said the people had locked the doors and were out. And we believed her. And all the time there were no people in the rooms at all.'

'And, my dears, she gave us her books, and they turn out to be all false.'

'Well, Harriet, Miss Amy Frost's account was correct, owing thirty-one shillings, and that we got.'

'*And that we got.* But that was all we got. Miss Leighton and Miss Jones, we paid her one hundred pounds down.'

'When we got in we found the house was empty.'

'But, dearest, that was not the worst of it.'

'No. This wretched woman – I can call her nothing else – had sold us furniture that was already sold. It was not hers to sell.'

'And now our lawyer has brought a bailiff to save other people from putting in bailiffs.'

'He thought, Miss Leighton, *his* bailiff would be likely to be a nicer kind of man than those put in by other creditors of the woman from whom we bought this house.'

'Harriet, dear, are we to feed him? Mr Rawlins, our lawyer, Miss Leighton and Miss Jones, tells us this man is an old soldier, and fought in the Crimean War, and has a medal.'

Emmie says she thought bailiffs always slept down-stairs with the cockroaches, and she is sure nobody ever fed them.

'But if he has a medal, Miss Jones. Harriet, dear, I think he must sleep on the sofa in the sitting room. We must give that room up to him altogether, and keep the door shut.'

Then Miss Lowe has a strange statement to make. She declares that whenever she speaks to this old man he calls her 'sir'!

At this Emmie and I can restrain ourselves no longer, and laugh heartily. Miss Lowe and Miss Greene join in.

Miss Lowe describes the situation with piquant melancholy.

'Mr Rawlins said, "Coombes, this is the mistress of the house. You take your orders from her." "Very good, sir," said he. Mr Rawlins went away. I said to the man, "Would you like a chair?" "Thank you, sir; I would, sir." I said, "You may sit on that one." "Thank you, sir," said he. And every time he has addressed or answered me since he has always called me "sir".'

'I can't understand it,' says Miss Greene, with her fore-head in a complicated pattern of wrinkles.

We can throw no light on the situation. It is our first acquaintance with a bailiff, a Crimean Medal, and a man who calls a woman 'sir'.

Miss Greene views the situation with more emotion than Miss Lowe, who naturally finds it impossible not to indulge in curiosity concerning a man who seems oblivi-ous of her gender, and with curiosity graver emotions refuse to run in harness. But while Miss Lowe exhibits a certain hardihood of manner towards their calamity, Miss

Greene retains a lively sense of its tearful nature. She takes out her handkerchief and blows her nose. After a certain age that operation is equal to wiping the eyes, but as dear Miss Greene is of uncertain age I cannot be really sure if that is what she is doing.

'I must let the other guests know,' she says. 'I must ask them to t-take no notice of a strange man they may see sitting in my sitting room.'

'Oh, dear Miss Greene, don't cry.'

'You are v-very kind, Miss J-Jones and Miss Leighton – I m-must.'

I say I see no reason why anyone need be told. But Miss Lowe says that if the guests were not informed by Miss Greene or herself that this strange man was a bailiff, someone from outside might tell them, and they might be afraid to remain in the house.

Miss Greene blows her nose again, and says there was s-something else. Would we m-mind very m-much if we d-did not l-let any v-visitors call and s-see us till *he* had g-gone? A g-glimpse of him m-might be caught in the hall, and he m-might be recognised.

This sounds as if our friends would probably be acquaintances of his, had probably shut him up in their own sitting rooms, but we overlook the impression.

'We will say we are out to everyone,' Emmie and I agree unanimously. 'Alice can tell them so at the front door.'

'It will not be for long, Miss Jones and Miss Leighton,' says Miss Lowe. 'I assure you it will not be for long.'

They express their gratitude. It is so very, *very* good of us. If all the guests are equally nice about it the worst of their trouble will be softened.

'And your friends will be saved any unpleasantness and shock,' adds Miss Greene.

Oh, yes. She is certainly convinced that our friends all know her bailiff.

When they have gone Emmie and I give way to giddy laughter. And Emmie then propounds a theory.

'How is it that you and I are always coming into contact with droll situations? Some people have nothing funny happen to them in a year. You and I, I believe, are smeared over with a magnetic fluid that attracts funny things towards us.'

'Like attracts like. You're rather quaint yourself, Em.'

The result of this interview is that we see nobody for a fortnight. We live in a state of barricade. *He* continues to make the sitting room his lair. Miss Greene and Miss Lowe continue to treat him with an unvarying courtesy and hospitality. And Miss Lowe continues to be addressed as 'sir'.

Gerald Huntley calls four times and then writes to ask if there is anything wrong.

'I ask because on my third and fourth call the housemaid said you were out before I had asked if you were in.'

And I can well imagine Alice opening the door with 'Hout' on her tongue, and letting it off before its release is requested. It is just what Alice would be sure to do. I write a little note and say we are in quarantine, that the disease is not dangerous, but is merely a slight financial trouble that has attacked Miss Greene and Miss Lowe. A letter comes next day asking can he do anything and begging to be allowed to see us for a minute. I write back that there is a tall man who served in the Crimea staying here, that he came without an invitation, that his presence hurts our tender-hearted landladies cruelly, and that it would hurt them still more if Mr Huntley or any stranger came in contact with their uninvited guest. Of course, I do not hint at Miss Greene's conviction that Mr Huntley and the man from the Crimea know each other well.

Sometimes Emmie and I overhear bits of conversation between the stranger and Miss Lowe as we come upstairs.

'Have you had sufficient dinner, Coombes?'

'Thank you kindly, sir; yes, sir.'

'Would you like the newspaper to read?'

'Thank you, sir; I would, sir. You're very good to me, you are, sir.'

'Well, I think you must be so lonely sitting here all day.'

'Well, sir, it is a bit quiet, sir; but it's what I'm used to now, sir.'

'Mr Rawlins tells me you served in the Crimean War, Coombes.'

'Yes, sir; indeed, I did, sir. Mr Rawlins has seen my medal, sir.'

'Well, Coombes, I must say you are very quiet and well-behaved for a – your occupation.'

'Thank you, sir. If there's anything I can do for you, sir, in the way of an odd job about the house, sir——'

'That *is* good of you, Coombes. Well, perhaps you would kindly help me to hang up some pictures in the dining room?'

'Certainly I will, sir.'

He gives a military salute each time he speaks to her. Big, fair, stolid Miss Lowe, with her husky voice and pronounced figure, has won him to her feet by sheer goodness of heart, in spite of his disregard of the fact that that same heart is feminine.

The barricade lasts a fortnight.

All that time Miss Greene and Miss Lowe go out a great deal and return looking tired and worried. They have numberless interviews with lawyers, agents, and business-people generally, and they find the woman who sold them the furniture and goodwill of this house is a trickster of much cunning. She had only been a fortnight in the house before she left, and had never paid for her own goodwill in it. She won over them to advance her a hundred pounds by declaring that she was about to undergo a terrible operation. And now she is away at Monte Carlo, and Miss Greene and Miss Lowe are learning a lesson in woman's wickedness that must surely sear a little the green of their fresh old hearts.

Emmie and I throw ourselves into our work. Spring urges and stimulates us. For three days I scarcely leave the piano. Emmie picks up any stray half-hour she can find on the music stool.

One night, worn out with a struggle with a Rubinstein concerto, I lie on the sofa looking out into the treetops. They are slowly, slowly coming into leaf, but oh, so slowly! For weeks the white pearls at the tips of the twigs seem to remain the same size.

I wish they would hurry. I long to see those pearls turn into leaves. At present I cannot think of them as anything but fruit blossoms. I expect to see the squares grow full of pink and white peach or apple blooms. It is because I have seen only fruit trees putting on their jewels for spring in Australia.

'Lay by my side your bunch of purple heather,' sings Emmie. I shut my eyes. I listen. I forget the trees, and the square, and Emmie, and the whole wide world. Everything fades except that voice singing.

In a trance I listen to her. It seems to me I never heard Emmie sing before. Her voice has always had a haunting, soulful timbre, but there was a coldness in her interpretation that her voice could not hide. 'You want your heart broken,' I used to say playfully – never thinking.

'Emmie! Emmie! You're *superb!* Emmie, you're *magnificent!* Emmie, you never sang like that before.'

'I suppose not,' says Emmie, in a low voice, coming over to the sofa. 'But, you see, my heart never was broken before.'

'Emmie!'

'Per is going back to Sweden.'

'Oh, Emmie!'

'He came one afternoon when you were out. I said goodbye. Sent him away.'

'But, Emmie, he was only a boy. You didn't care. And he was a Swede.'

'I know. He was only a boy. He was only a Swede, and I would never marry any man that was not English or Australian. But his blue eyes, his blue eyes ...'

Well, Emmie can sing with anybody now.

The barricade ends at last. Mr Rawlins arranges affairs with a master hand, and a day comes when the sitting room is empty of a tall old man in navy blue, and Miss Lowe comes back to her lost womanhood.

That same night another elderly gentleman arrives, but he addresses Miss Lowe as Harriet, and Miss Lowe apostrophises him as Papa. He is a country businessman who has lost his fortune, and now lives frugally with his wife and her sister in a cottage in Surrey, while his daughter fights for their bread up here in London. Emmie and I are invited down to meet him. What a long, lingering, protracted, tearful, pathetic story the two ladies have been telling him.

'If I had known what these poor girls had been going through,' says he.

'Papa, you were not intended to know,' says the youngest girl. The elder one is exhausted with her narrative, and merely nods her feelings.

He asks us what *we* think of the departed warrior. It is as profound a problem to him as to us that his daughter should be addressed as 'sir'.

'I can't make it out at all,' says he, slowly sipping the hot drink his devoted Harriet has mixed for him. 'Can't understand it at all. Didn't he know the difference between the sexes?'

His left eye winks just then, not because it wants to, but because he suffers from a nervous falling of the eyelid. Emmie coughs. He puts his finger in his waistcoat pocket and draws out a gelatine lozenge. 'Allow me to present you with a lozenge, Miss,' says he.

But do you think gelatines would take away the tickling in Emmie's mental apparatus? Before we can be healed of our laughter we must forget that here in the same house with us dwell these amusing characters whose simplicity, originality and unworldliness have taught us that not even great, big, wicked, worldly London, not even keeping an apartment house in London, can rob some women of their everlasting childhood and innocence.

And I put the bailiff along with the little man in the train. It may be some day I shall solve the problem of them both. Till then …

Emmie is singing magnificently. She cries at night to herself now. And in the daytime she sings so that the agents forgive her being an Australian. The Dog's Life is open to her. She has a two years' engagement.

Alfred and Jean may be back any day.

It makes me sad to think this is all going to pass away soon, this dear, deep, student life in the City of Mists. Australia is still Australia. I am faithful to her in every bone and fibre. When I think of her an impression of dazzling wealth flashes across my brain, and an intoxicating odour of gum trees steals powerfully over my senses, and I grow dizzy with happiness at the sight and scent of my country.

But London is stronger. London drives out the gums. London hangs pictures, and plays, and cathedrals, and operas, and intellects all over the Bush and the dazzling gold. And I say to myself, in unmistakable language, 'I don't want to go back. It's so far, far away. It's the other end of the world. I don't want to go back yet.'

It is not only the London-ness of London that has me prisoner. It is its nearness to other places. Can you understand that it is a few *hours* to Paris, to Holland, to Ireland, and Scotland! I could not believe it at first. Think of this. I can get to Greece – yes, there really is a place called Greece – more quickly than you can get to Perth.

The wonderful nearness of so many great places bewilders an Antipodean brain. We cannot realise that you can get *anywhere* in a few hours. It seems to us as if there *must* be weeks between Ireland and Scotland. I always imagined myself taking about fourteen days to get to France, a month to Russia, and to travel to Norway and Sweden required something less than a year in my thoughts.

When we think of these places we see the globe lying between them and us. That great distance is always in our travels. When the nearness of the Continent becomes clear to us we feel that to live in London is just the same as to live in France, Italy, Germany. Any place that can be reached in thirty-six hours appears to be almost on our property. When I wake in the morning and think 'I am in London,' I think also, 'and in Paris and Holland, and Germany and Switzerland.'

And so, London means everywhere to us. To leave London and go back means to leave all Europe also. Even if we never get there, we always can – as long as we are in England. But go back to Australia and the whole world vanishes, like a dream, and becomes, after a time, only a dream again.

Your living

SILVER.

CHAPTER XVII

DEAR EVERYBODY,

I feel like a great discoverer. Suddenly I have discovered all I have discovered. It lies round me in shining stretches. And I am rich, rich, rich, beyond the dreams of avarice.

But first let me tell you it's a spring day, and London is a poem in pale green trees and white houses newly painted, and twittering birds and sunlight, and a dancing rhythm of hurrying feet and bright voices and happy intentions, and cool, clear air, and the great strong pulse of spring beating from streets and squares all over the city. Am I in *London*? Is it not the Bush that lies away beyond my window? The little trees are in exquisite green. But the big ones haven't changed yet. They flash up bare and black still from the undergrowth of gay young things beneath them, and the square is not the square. It is a vista in a world of gum trees. The young green trees are the baby eucalyptus of my home. The big bare ones are ring-barked gums. Only one thing is missing – the poignant, subtle, sad, delirious odour of the gums. Nothing is like it here. It is not even ever so dimly imitated by any of the tree or flower scents stealing through the streets of London.

Do you know what Emmie does? Don't tell the Bush, will you? It mightn't like it. She goes out into Hyde Park, that looks like paddocks in the early morning, and lies on the grass under the plane trees, and crumples up a gumleaf sent her from home in a letter, and shuts her eyes and buries her nose in the crumpled leaf, and inhales and sniffs and sighs and pretends and imagines and nearly believes she is lying on Australian grass under Australian trees.

This is not homesickness. If Emmie could go home now she would not. Her roots have taken here. She feels the fascination of the Old World working in her blood, fighting the Australian corpuscles. She tells me sometimes that Sydney is a little, quiet, ignorant, provincial town, and she can never live there again, and she does not want to live there again, and she does not intend to live there again, and she doesn't know how anyone can ever go back there to live again, and she doesn't know how she ever lived there so long.

To which I add, 'Or how London ever lived without you?'

'You can be as sarcastic as you please. I'm a celebrated singer now and too stupid to understand you.'

No. It is not homesickness that makes us sniff hungrily at the bits of boronia and wild Bush things you send in letters. It is mean, *au fond*. I hardly like to confess. Truth is, while we break up the gumleaves and bury our noses in the subtle aroma we are filled with an exquisite emotion: our bodies are here in London, but the scent of Australia is stealing to our brain. That is the most beautiful scent in the world to us. Our whole land is blown with it. I fancy, if we ever come back, we will begin to feel it when we get within a hundred miles of Australia. But it can never give so subtle a sensation over there as here in London. It takes us away yet leaves us here. *Yet leaves us here!* There's where the meanness of our gum-worship comes in. We, in London, like to get drunk with the scent of Australia – over there. We want to worship and stay away.

These are my three delusions:

I thought I could never have any friends in London. I thought people would shut their doors quickly. I thought the people that lived in houses lived miles away from London.

I thought everyone would think, 'What a frightful accent you have!'

I thought the English never asked anyone to come and see them. In Australia it is always said, 'You'll find the English so cold and unfriendly.' That argues a want of sense on Australians' parts. It is not friendly or unfriendly to invite people quickly, to gush over them immediately. It is neither warm nor cold. At heart the friendliness lies. And at heart, if we had the sense to see it, the friendliness *is*, among these new English people. It is just as kindly a friendliness as ours to strangers, and it goes on growing. At home it is a common thing to see friendships grow up in an hour. To see a sudden burst of interest given and returned, to see a sudden exhausted flickering, followed by total extinction. Such friendships are very common among us. We think ourselves warmer than the English, but are we?

I have now an English girlfriend, Lucy Netteridge. It was so difficult, that friendship, in its beginning. It seemed to me we were always working against something.

I couldn't see friendship coming at all. I could see Lucy gradually, gradually, becoming a little more interested in me, but not more pliant. She began to come to see me. I wondered why. She didn't make me feel she liked me. She told me scarcely anything about herself. But she continued to come at intervals. And I went to see her at intervals. No progress seemed to be made. We made talk all the time. There were no confidences, no giving or taking. I was 'Miss Leighton'. She was 'Miss Netteridge'. It seemed as if we would never get any nearer. I was interested in her. She was a study to me, so self-possessed, so marked, so prim, and considerate, and gentle, with such a delightful voice. I admired her intensely. But I was never sorry when she had gone. There was a consciousness of my brain getting free again, of the blood flowing more easily through the capillaries when I got away from her. And yet we went on and on. It was her way, I suppose. I was following her lead. We went on and on, and all of a sudden one afternoon I found that here was a real, real friendship, here was a beautiful girl with a deep, strong nature, well-hidden, become my friend, and taking me for hers. And all the boredom that had belonged to the early stages of our acquaintance fled. We had sown our tame oats. Now we could be happy together.

Honest confession: I'm getting English. I never knew it till today, till I went to an Australian party. Then I found myself shrinking back from what I had been longing for so often – the gay, free chatter, the unstinted expressions of welcome, of my fellow countrymen.

I fear I have grown old and dull. There was something irritating to me in confronting those Australians *en masse*. I missed something to lean up against, something one gradually comes to need – the restraint and reserve of the English. It is such an excuse for being dull.

The air seemed full of hysterical exclamations. Everyone talked at once. Our nervous energy must be enormous. We pour it out like water. That is why an Australian party is so fatiguing. Everyone gives so much, and so much is demanded of you. Some conversation:

'How do you like London?'

'I think it's lovely.'

'What do you think of the people?'

'Well——'

'Are you going back to Australia?'

'Oh! I hope not. I feel I could never live there again.'

'Neither could I. My husband will have to come over here and live. He says he can't, but he must.'

'I can't understand how anyone can ever go back there to live after living here.'

'London's so wonderful. You can get everything in London. But don't you think it's rather *slow*?'

'In doing things? Oh, yes, frightfully slow. London takes such a long time to know what it means. Last week I went to hire a gas stove for my new flat. I expected to have it sent home in a few hours, of course. Well, I had to interview one man after another, to sign paper after paper, to state who had had the flat before, and where he lived, and tell all about his gas affairs, and who I was, far back into my past, and who the previous occupants of the flat were, far back into *their* past; and even then I didn't get my stove. They kept me waiting ten whole days. That was the custom. Their stoves are so tied up with red tape that it takes ten days to undo them.'

'In Sydney one does business straight off.'

'And are not these trams and 'buses slow? Think of our little electric trams flying along. We think we are frightfully behind the times out there. We have to come to London to learn how wonderfully advanced we are.'

'I think we have too little conceit. We are all brought up with the idea that we're only Australians. We look on the English as a far superior race to us in every way. Then, when we come here, we are surprised at many things. Because we read poetry ourselves we think England must read it doubly much. It doesn't. The only people who care about it here are those who write it.'

'But still I'd rather live in London than anywhere in the world.'

'Oh, yes, so would I!'

And so would I.

Your loving

SYLVIA.

CHAPTER XVIII

LONDON, *April* 190—.

MY DARLING MOTHER,

Oh, to be in England now that April's here!

You will all realise to the full the mad, glad luxury to me of saying that to myself and then going to my window to look out into the square. Do you remember, Peg, how we used to croon those words to ourselves away in the Bush, up the North Shore line, trying and straining to call up the picture – but in vain?

April's here, and I am in England, and the streets are full of flowers. For a penny you can have daffodils enough to fill your rooms with gold. And the trees are breaking into green. For six months they have looked as if a great ushfire had swept over them all and burnt the last flicker of life out of them. It was impossible to believe they were not dead.

I loved them black, because they looked to me like gum trees charred by a wild, fierce fire.

Now they are going to grow into great, fat, green, placid trees, and everybody will admire and love them, so they will not notice if my affection wanes a little.

'Oh! to be in England,' and to have come from Australia, and to see the crate of flowers standing in front of our fireplace this very minute.

It came this morning, to mark the dolorous fact that I am twenty-two today. There was no card, but I guess who sent it. I went into raptures over just such a basket one day lately, and the sender was present, so I hold him guilty.

If you could see the enormity of the basket you would not think guilty too big a word. It is like a Chinaman's basket, such as they carry at the end of a pole in Sydney. It is nearly as high as my waist, and is filled to the brim with daffodils, white tulips, yellow tulips, wallflowers, red roses, golden roses, jonquils, that dart their arrowy odour through the brain till you could faint with the delicious pain, great purple flag-lilies, great white lilies, masses of poignant purple hyacinths, till the ecstasy of colour that leaps into our dingy sitting room brings tears into my eyes.

Purple flowers have a strange intensity of expression that always compels me. That a flower should be purple seems contrary to the laws of nature. It is a colour that nature rarely uses. Sometimes she vouchsafes to veil a high mountain in it, to fill a noble gully with it, but this is a soft and evanescent purple that changes into blue even as you look at it. To capture or keep purple is not a common trick of hers. And when I see purple flowers I am at once arrested. They strike a note of imperial cruelty that rings straight down into my subconsciousness. I neither love them nor hate them, because I never have the opportunity to know them well enough. But I wake when I see them, and I always have to think about them when they come my way.

And the basket is lined with thin purple paper, and the irises and hyacinths are deeper than ever against it.

To have more flowers than you want is one of the few tolerable overabundances of this life. Too much money would compel you to worry over your will. Too much love would be a bore. Too much brain would be boring to other people. But too many flowers would be easily supportable. They would be gone before they tired you.

I kneel down and bury my head in the crate. I love to be almost rough to flowers, to press my face hard against them, trying to steal their wonderful, ineffable secret of youth and happiness going side by side with pain and decay, and as sad as joyful, as merry as serious.

While I am kneeling someone comes into the room. I look up and see a big, big man in grey.

'Is anything the matter?' he asks.

'How do you do? Nothing at all. How *could* anything be the matter when *these* are in the room?'

'I am glad to see you are out of quarantine again.'

'*He* went away last night.'

'How are the maiden ladies?'

'As nice and well and funny as ever.'

'Won't you let me get you a chair?'

'I want to stay down here near this. But you may sit down, won't you?'

'I am not sure whether I have come to stay.'

'Em and I are not going out, and Miss Greene will be in in a minute. I asked her to come and have some of my flowers. Selfishness. I wanted to have them all over the house, and she is a dear.'

'Is she?'

'She takes good care of us. "I pride myself," says she, "on a house where mothers can leave their daughters, and husbands their wives."' I never can help imitating Miss Greene's voice, and really, considering with what lingering appreciation she mouths her syllables and adorns and points and punctuates her sentiments, it is no unworthy speech I imitate.

The big man in grey with grey eyes answers, without laughing, 'And what about husbands? Can they be left here too?'

'How solemnly you ask! You haven't got a wife who wants to leave you somewhere, have you?'

'No, I haven't. I haven't. But...'

But I cannot go any further. I have gone the very, *very* furthest. I didn't see it coming, truly. But it *came*. And it's it.

I can't write any more.

Jean and Alfred will be home this week. What will Jean say? What will Alfred say? What will you all say?

Gerald says that since all roads lead to Rome it is not so *very* wonderful that he had to go there to find ME.

And to think it should all end like this – music, flowers, trees, city, glamour, pictures – all ending in Man. It's a termination common to all languages. And yet, I suppose, it always strikes a girl with surprise when she first finds it at the end of all her substantives.

But already it seems the best end. If all these beautiful things are not to lead us to human beings, the nearest images of Christ, what would the gayest, brightest life be worth? There is only one blot on my happiness – that two men can ask one woman to marry them, and Mrs Vosges is English, and so nice too, and I'm only an Australian.

But I can't write, I'm just your little, littlest

SILVER.

THE END

GRATTAN STREET PRESS PERSONNEL

Semester 1, 2018

Editing and Proofreading
Grayce Arlov, Ellie Atack, Luke Fussell, Jessica Hall,
Stephanie Lightfoot, Beth Wentworth

Design and Production
Ellen Dutton, Angela Iaria, Alexandra Robson, Beth
Wentworth

Sales and Marketing
Jessica Allan, Brooke Munday, Audrey Whybrow

Social Media
Cherry Cai, Georgia Gallo

Submissions Officers
Ellie Atack, Laura Bianca Cesile, Katie Hollister, Sunniva
Midtskogen, Audrey Whybrow

Website and Blogs
Georgia Quirke-Luping, Laura Bianca Cesile, Katie
Hollister, Sunniva Midtskogen

Academic Staff
Mark Davis, Katherine Day, Aaron Mannion, Sybil Nolan.

ACKNOWLEDGEMENTS

This semester we raised the bar by publishing two books in the Colonial Australian Popular Fiction series simultaneously. Congratulations and thanks to the students involved in the editing and production, who rose brilliantly to the challenge: Ellen Dutton and Alexandra Robson (production editors and typesetters); Grayce Arlov, Luke Fussell, Jessica Hall and Stephanie Lightfoot (editors and proofreaders); and Angela Iaria (design and paging). Thanks also to the rest of the Grattan Street Press team, who checked OCR scans against the original texts and made corrections.

We are grateful to academic staff in the Master of Publishing and Communications who assisted the project: Mark Davis (who created the original design for the series, and gave helpful advice on its implementation), Aaron Mannion (who oversaw GSP last year, and gave us valuable advice on workflow), and Katherine Day (who always seemed to be there when editorial help and advice was needed).

We are also grateful to our new Head of School, Professor Jennifer Milam, for her support; to Beth Driscoll, David McInnis and Maria Tumarkin, and other academic staff who gave advice and assistance; to Annemarie Levin who helped us on an almost daily basis to process sales through our website and to source services; to Amanda Morris at the Australian Centre, for advice about the launch; and to GSP alumni Bianca Jafari and Wes Whitfield, who helped out in various ways between and/or during semester.

Thanks also to Ken Gelder and Rachael Weaver for their responsiveness as series editors, and their continuing interest in both the colonial fiction project and the Press itself. And last but not least, thanks to Debbie Lee, Rushelle Lister, and the rest of the staff at our printers, IngramSpark.

Sybil Nolan, Coordinator, Grattan Street Press

ABOUT GRATTAN STREET PRESS

Grattan Street Press is a trade publisher based in Melbourne. A start-up press, we aim to publish a range of work, including contemporary literature, trade non-fiction, and children's books, and to re-publish culturally valuable works that are out of print. The press is an initiative of the Publishing and Communications program in the School of Culture and Communication at the University of Melbourne, and is staffed by graduate students, who receive hands-on experience of every aspect of the publication process.

The press is a not-for-profit organisation that seeks to build long-term relationships within the Australian literary and publishing community. We also partner with community organisations in Melbourne and beyond to co-publish books that contribute to public knowledge and discussion.

Organisations interested in partnering with us can contact us at coordinator@grattanstreetpress.com.

ABOUT THE AUSTRALIAN CENTRE

The Australian Centre is based in the School of Culture and Communication at the University of Melbourne, with Professor Ken Gelder and Professor Denise Varney as its co-directors. It aims to develop innovative research projects in the Australian arts and humanities across a range of disciplines, including Art History, Theatre Studies, Literary Studies, Cultural Studies, Media and Communication, Cinema Studies, Indigenous Studies and Creative Writing.